# SONG
# OF
# ROLAND

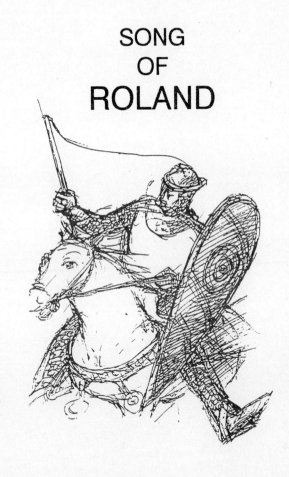

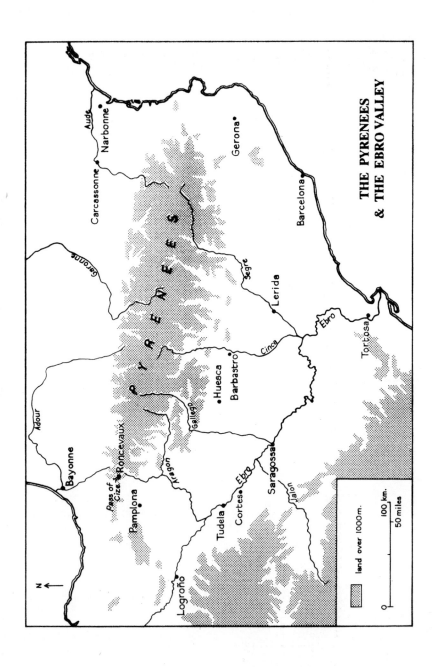

THE PYRENEES
& THE EBRO VALLEY

land over 1000m.

100 km.
50 miles

# SONG
## OF
# ROLAND

translated with an introduction
by
JANET SHIRLEY

First published in 1996
by Llanerch Publishers,
Felinfach.
Copyright © Janet Shirley, 1996.

ISBN 1 86143 005 1

# INTRODUCTION

# Introduction

Somewhere about nine hundred years ago a poet of the greatest
genius sat down to bring an old story up to date. His material was a
defeat suffered in the Pyrenees by Charles king of the Franks in the
year 778 AD, and this he transformed into the famous epic of Roland
and Oliver, of their betrayal by Ganelon, their death in battle and the
revenge taken for them by their lord Charlemagne, the mighty
emperor. How far legend had already been at work on this story, the
exact form of the material when he took it in hand, we shall never
know. We can however be certain that neither the author nor his
audiences would have been in the least impressed if a pedantic
time-traveller from our own day were to return to them to point out
the discrepancies between eighth century fact and eleventh or twelfth
century fiction. In the *Roland* Charlemagne appears as the God-sent
scourge of the Moslems and conqueror of the entire landmass of
Spain, whereas in sober truth he conducted an inconclusive campaign
in northern Spain as the ally of a Moslem emir. In the poem it is the
wicked heathen who swoop down and slaughter the unhappy
rearguard, but in August 778 it was the mountain-dwelling Basques
who ambushed and looted Charles's baggage-train as it returned to
France. The dead included a Frankish noble called Roland, the
emperor's commander of the borders between France and Brittany.

But the *Roland* poet was not writing history. He was using this
episode as a foundation for his masterpiece, whose purpose it was to
affirm and celebrate the theme then very much in the air, *Gesta dei
per francos*, the things God has done through the Franks.

The Franks or French of the early twelfth century were
peculiarly certain that they were God's own special combat troops. It

i

is a conviction not restricted to that time or that nation. In other ways, though, we in our largely post-Christian world find it hard to understand the common assumptions of that period. It was a time when God and his saints in heaven were thought of as individual powers to be reckoned with. So too were the devils in hell. Conversion of unbelievers was a duty, and if they refused to convert they were obviously better dead.

It was a violent age, one of expansionist warfare and especially of crusades. Even the invasion of England in 1066 ranked as a holy war and was blessed by the pope. The first crusade against Moslem powers in the Middle East began in 1096. After unimaginable hardships Godfrey of Bouillon in 1099 took the title of Advocate of Jerusalem (he refused to be a king and wear a golden crown in the city where Christ had worn a crown of thorns) and the Latin kingdom of Jerusalem began its precarious existence.

Long before this, though, beginning as early as 1018, Christian warriors had been going from all parts of France to help their fellow-believers in Spain to resist and even push back the tide of Moslem advance. Inspired by the Cluniac revival, churchmen and laymen sent monks, settlers and campaigners into Navarre, Aragon and Catalonia. Links between rulers in southern France and northern Spain were close, especially at the Mediterranean end of the Pyrenean chain, and so too were links between churches.

The most effective campaigns in these parts took place between 1064 and 1120, just the period from which the *Roland* is thought to come. And we cannot doubt that the poem was written by a man who knew the dangerous passes through the Pyrenees, knew the heat and exhaustion of a long day in armour under the Spanish sun, the rushing mountain torrents and the deep swift Ebro, the yew trees, olives, pines and tall beeches, the green meadows and the bright red flowers that blossomed where the heroes' blood had fallen. The vivid detail of the poem puts it beyond question; he was describing what he knew.

Many of his audience would have known these things too. The knights who listened to him over their evening meal would include veterans who had fought across that ground and faced those enemies. Perhaps they or their fathers had been present at the fall of Barbastro in 1065 or had seen their friends die at Zalaca near Badajoz in 1086, when the roll of the terrifying Berber drums was first heard in Spain. They might have laboured in the siege of Huesca in Aragon in 1096, or in the seven-month siege and capture of Saragossa in 1118, when Gaston de Béarn of Jerusalem fame, Rotrou du Perche of Normandy and Gaston Guillaume the fighting bishop of Pamplona led the Christian forces to victory. This is why the nugget of historical fact provided by Charlemagne's expedition of 778 served the *Roland* author's purpose so well. It not only gave him a heroic champion of the Christian faith for his principal figure, it also offered a setting for his story which would awaken the liveliest memories in his hearers. One can imagine them sitting there and echoing the warcry 'Mountjoy!' with which several sections conclude, or taking a well-informed interest in technical details - swords of Viana steel, a helmet from Provence, the exact make of a good shield, the best kind of warhorse, the type of blow needed to kill an opponent in just the way described - they hiss the villains, applaud the heroes and shout hearty approval, we can be sure, whenever their own racial group comes in for mention. Incidentally we may note that it is undoubtedly the Franks of France who get star billing. Normans, Bretons, Saxons, Frisians and all the rest, they are brave and warlike men, excellent comrades in a tight place, but it is the French who ride with the emperor himself, the French against whom no enemy can stand. This need not mean that the author was himself a Frank, only that this version of the poem was written for Frankish audiences.

CONTENT AND STYLE OF THE POEM

It is important to remember that the title we use for this work, the 'Song of Roland', is a modern one. We do not know what its author called it - perhaps the 'Song of Roncevaux' or the 'Vengeance of Charlemagne'. Roland himself dies less than half way through the poem, and the overall theme is much larger than the calamity that hits one man. It is a story of courage, of treachery, of pride leading to disaster, of brothers in arms whose lives depend on each other's loyalty, and above all of the triumph of good over evil. Heathen may intrigue, false Ganelon may betray, but great Charles, symbol and channel of God's power, will see that right prevails. Great Charles, hammer of the heathen, is an old old man in tears half the time, helpless without sensible Duke Naimon to tell him what to do next and the angel Gabriel to help him do it, without God himself to avert the enemy's blow. He is a most interesting study of the limitations of mortal man, of God's power made manifest in weakness. He not only defeats Marsile, the Moslem threat, he does better than that and crushes the great Emir Baligant, risen from the depths of the pagan past, older than Homer and Virgil. Classical antiquity itself goes down before the champion of Christ.

The story is told in just over 4,000 ten-syllable lines of verse. These lines do not rhyme but are assonanced in groups of varying length, groups now usually called 'laisses'. The lengths vary, partly because a sound that is difficult to assonance will naturally give a shorter laisse, but also because the length of a laisse is adapted to its content. They are real units, not arbitrary subdivisions of the text. This is especially evident with the 'laisses similaires', the groups of stanzas in which it seems at first glance that the poet is carelessly repeating himself, sometimes twice, sometimes three times. He even appears once to contradict himself, in Roland's famous double reply to his stepfather Ganelon (laisses 59 and 60), the first reply exquisitely courteous, the second savage in its brutality. But these repetitions are perfectly deliberate. Our poet was not a dear old simpleton who could not tell the difference between once and twice. He was a most accomplished artist. The laisses similaires serve several purposes: they allow room for text and subtext to be developed, they heighten tension, and above all they enable the performer to show his audience, not just to tell them, what was taking place. See for example laisses 28-30 and then 40-41, in which devious Ganelon and first Blancandrin then Marsile are shown edging cautiously towards an understanding. The laisses similaires also serve a purely practical purpose in that they make sure the audience does not miss important points. No one was going to sit down quietly and read this work to himself; it would be heard, it would be watched, probably in a busy baronial hall with servants and others coming and going, dogs suddenly squabbling, a messenger arriving, and now and then someone throwing fresh logs on the fire.

This is a supremely important point: the story was not simply recited, it was performed, it was a drama. The narrator did not just stand there and chant or declaim it, he gave it, he acted it. With the help of a few props - a sword, a cloak, an ivory horn, perhaps a crown - he would present the whole mighty drama, taking each part in turn - brave Roland, wise Oliver, great Charles, and the traitor Ganelon, smooth-spoken, so handsome that none could take their eyes off him. The text is full of dialogue, very direct, meant to be spoken, and of sudden changes of mood, inexplicable lying there flat on the page, but crystal clear on the lips of a performer.

Whether the author of this text also performed it is one of the many things we do not know. It is so brilliantly composed, so playable, that it is hard not to think of its creator as a man like Shakespeare, one who knew his craft from every angle. But we know really nothing about him. His name may have been Thorold, in Latin Turoldus, a not uncommon name at that time in France, Normandy and England, but then again it may not. A Turoldus is mentioned in the last line of the poem, but we do not know whether this is the poet signing off, or a reference to some earlier work on which his own is based.

### THE MANUSCRIPT DIGBY 23

The earliest manuscript we possess is not the original nor even a copy of the original; it is thought to be a copy of a copy of it, and a poor one at that. It was made perhaps in the middle of the twelfth century, 'is by no means well written and contains many errors' (Whitehead p. v). It was subsequently touched up by a would-be corrector whose 'gross ignorance' Whitehead deplores. This manuscript is the famous Digby 23 in the Bodleian library in Oxford. It lay there unknown until it was discovered in the early nineteenth century and an edition of it was published in 1837. Very many other manuscript versions of the story exist, in French, in Franco-Italian, in Middle High German, Old Norse and other languages, but Digby 23 in spite of its faults is far and away the earliest and the noblest version we have. The language used is 'Western French of the early twelfth century, with a slight Anglo-Norman colouring most probably due to the scribe' (Whitehead p. xiii).

### DATE OF COMPOSITION

The date of the poem's composition is hotly disputed, some putting it as early as 1066, others as late as 1120. The question is too complex to go into here and readers must pursue it for themselves with the help of the bibliography.

## SOME PROBLEMS

As we said earlier, it is difficult, indeed impossible, for us to enter into the feelings of a twelfth century audience. We know so many things they did not, and we are ignorant of so much they took for granted. When Ganelon, for instance, rides into camp very early in the morning as dawn is breaking, we may think, ah, what a striking picture, but the contemporary audience would instantly have picked up the unspoken reference to the morning star, Lucifer, light-bringer, once the fairest of the angels, now a prince of the devils in hell. And as they listened to that traitor's brilliant fictions, they would have remembered who it was that was 'a liar and the father of it' and 'a murderer from the beginning' (St John's Gospel viii 44). They accepted, too, the efficacy of prayer. When the archbishop declared that men who cannot bear arms must become monks and pray - 'pray for our sins', he says, not for their own, for ours that as soldiers we cannot help committing - they would have understood that he expected those men to carry on the war against evil on another and valid front. They would also have recognised the crusading and other references over which scholars now labour. Besides this, they would have known other stories in the same canon, now lost, and would have recognised Walter, count of Hum, who merely puzzles us, and would not have needed telling that Ganelon had married Charlemagne's widowed sister, who was also Roland's mother. They would have known, as we never shall, just why those two men hated each other.

Another difficulty for a modern reader is the author's cheerful disregard for historical accuracy. Here he is, as we saw earlier, blithely describing eighth century events in twelfth century terms. But we ought to be used to this: does not Shakespeare have the murderers of Julius Caesar listening anxiously to a striking clock? And we have seen that our poet had a purpose: he was using eighth century events to create a twelfth century story. But he has the same attitude to other cultures as well and describes other races in terms of his own people. It is disconcerting to open the book and find the Moslem king talking about 'sweet France'; we do not expect the enemy to speak like this. Queen Bramimonde, his consort, behaves exactly like a noble Frankish lady, delivering gifts and gracious words to the man her lord is pleased to honour. Surely, we think, a Moslem ruler's wife would have been safely shut away with her colleagues in the harem? But we have to accept that this was the literary convention of the day. As Southern says, 'Men inevitably shape the world they do not know in the likeness of the world they do know' (*Western Views*, p.32). Other times and other places appear in contemporary manners and dress. As our author said of another matter: What else should they do?

A difficult area for us in this respect is that of religion. Fighting Archbishop Turpin who wielded so strong a lance and died so well, what was he doing shedding so much blood in so unchristian a way? But this is a naive reaction on our part. Now as then, Christ's commands of love and forgiveness are set aside as impracticable more often than not. And the memory of Moslem massacres in Spain and France was then still vivid, the threat still urgent. This was a time when bishops did take arms and fight to defend their flocks; Boissonnade approvingly cites several, both French and Spanish (see bibliography). Adhémar bishop of Le Puy was an invaluable commander in the First Crusade, and Odo bishop of Bayeux is plain to be seen on the Bayeux Tapestry ready to bring his mace down on the nearest English head. It is also true to say that Turpin's role in this work is symbolic: he stands for Holy Church battling against the powers of darkness.

What we cannot excuse, can only find repulsive, is the blatantly false picture our author gives of the Moslem and Jewish faiths. A synagogue or a mosque was the last place in the world in which to find graven images, and yet the victorious Franks are shown cleaning up Saragossa and overthrowing idols in mosques and synagogues (laisse 272). And Moslems are shown as idolaters, as polytheists, bowing down in prayer to images of Mahomet, Apollin and the mysterious Tervagant. Did our author not know that Mahomet's great message was that God is One, and that Moslems considered idolatry so abominable that representations of the human form found almost no place in their art? He did know that a Moslem king's bedroom might be adorned with written decoration - 'painted and inscribed with many colours'. (laisse 188). He knew that Moslem 'clergy' differed from those of the Christian church in having neither tonsure nor orders (laisse 270). But in general Christendom at the turn of the eleventh and twelfth centuries knew very little about Islam, only that it was dangerous. Needing to produce a picture of a rival faith, it was natural to our author to offer nothing better than a parody of his own religion. He did not invent it; it was an accepted convention of his time.

### The Present Translation

French of this period was still in some ways close to its original Latin. It was a language of great flexibility and of the terse vigour which derived from the use of a strong, spare vocabulary and, in the case of the *Roland* poet, from genius. This was a man who could achieve any effect he wanted - glory, pathos, horror - in a minimum of words. Translating him is all but blasphemous. I have tried to be accurate, and especially to make clear the supreme importance of what can loosely be called the feudal spirit - the mutual duty and mutual faith which operated both vertically (lord to man and man to lord) and horizontally (comrade to comrade). This permeates the text but is easy to lose in translation.

Editions used begin with Bédier and include all the later ones; see bibliography. I have followed Whitehead's order and numbering of the laisses, but not always his reading of the manuscript. Conjectural translations of lost or illegible phrases are shown by square brackets, gaps in the manuscript by a line of dots. Words in italic are those whose meaning is not known. Asterisks refer to notes at the back of the book.

### NEW INSIGHTS OFFERED IN THIS TRANSLATION

These include light shed by the great dictionary-maker Cotgrave on the meaning of the word *exill*, which in laisses 140 and 211 is said to have struck the land of France. This is generally taken to mean some general ruin or disaster, but Cotgrave quite precisely says: 'Exilment de pais. The dispeopling of a country'. What Roland and Charlemagne respectively are mourning is the loss to France of her sons, her fighting men. Another new interpretation is that of the word *brandir*. Often it clearly means 'to brandish', but on five occasions the victor is said to 'brandish his blow' as part of the killing process (laisses 93, 95, 118, 146, 293). Here, from the context, it must mean that the attacker, having embedded his weapon in his enemy's body, knocks him over sideways with a strong lateral thrust.

For a fresh interpretation of the word *espaneliz* in laisse 192, see the note to that laisse and the light cast by a phrase written by William Golding.

### OTHER PROBLEMS OF TRANSLATION

One is the reluctant loss of the distinction between *tu* and *vous*. The *vous* form is surprisingly common, even between dearest friends at the tenderest moments. The use of *tu* indicated one's own superiority as much as anything else, as indeed it still can, and no one, for example, ever addresses the emperor as *tu* except the archangel Gabriel, a heathen messenger trying to insult him, and the great Emir Baligant in the last battle. *Tu* is also used in the formal prayers to God, closely based on Latin models. The author moves freely between the *tu* and *vous* forms of the verbs as his metre demands, even within a single sentence addressed to one person. He also switches from one tense to another at will. The present and the present perfect are common and are used with strong dramatic effect. My use of tenses in English does not reflect that of the original.

One unresolved problem is that of the purpose of the letters *aoi* written rather large in the righthand margins of the manuscript, usually near the end of a laisse. They occur some 179 times, according to no pattern we can now discern. Theories as to their purpose are as abundant as slaughtered heathen on the field of battle: Are they stage-directions, exclamations, instructions to musicians, prayers? No one knows. See bibliography, especially Duggan, for a host of fascinating speculations.

Two problem phrases: *tere majur* is here translated as the 'Great Land', ie the kingdom of France and its dependent territories, but it may well mean the 'land of our forebears'. *Outremer* literally means 'beyond the sea' and often but not always refers to the Holy Land.

The expression 'seven': this number occurs frequently, either on its own or as part of a larger figure - seven years in Spain, seven hundred camels, a thousand and seven hundred blows - and must be meant to indicate 'a very large number'.

Jewels are often mentioned and warriors on both sides blazed with gems. They were not only signs of wealth and therefore of power but were also thought to have intrinsic efficacy. Some shone with their own light, like the carbuncles that lit the Emir's fleet on its way across the dark sea, others protected against loss of blood, drunkenness, snake-bite, and so on. Thus the infidels' glittering shields and helmets were not merely rich and gorgeous but full of devilish magic.

The *Geste francor* - laisses 112 and 240 refer listeners to the authority of the *Geste francor*, an echo of such titles as *Gesta francorum et aliorum hierosolymitanum* and *Gesta francorum Jerusalem expugnantium*, 'Deeds of the Franks and others who went to Jerusalem' and 'Deeds of the Franks who took Jerusalem' respectively. We do not know if our poet is referring to a particular text or just using a learned phrase to lend respectability to his claims.

The word *geste*, from the Latin *gesta*, 'things done', occurs several times in the Roland. In laisse 63 Roland refuses to accept reinforcements because he will not *la geste en desment*, 'give the lie to the record'. In laisse 155 the numbers killed by Turpin in his last stand are said to be recorded by the *geste* and by St Giles. The Emir Baligant remarks in laisse 232 that Charles' courage is recorded in several *gestes*. In laisse 227 the poet refers to the authority of *l'anciene geste*. Finally there is the famous last line of the poem with its ambiguous *Ci falt la geste que Turoldus declinet*. *Ci falt* means 'here ends', *la geste* 'the record' or 'story', but controversy rages over the meaning of the last three words. *Que* can mean 'which' or 'because'. *Turoldus*, perhaps Thorold, may be the author or a source he is referring to, or even a scribe. *Declinet* is used in laisse 179 of the approach of evening, night 'falls'; it can also mean 'to narrate' or 'to end' or can indicate poor health.

## THE NAMES

Names are given not only to people and horses but to swords and spears as well. I have translated some but not all of these. Many of the infidels have names beginning with Mal, 'evil', so that Malquiant son of Malcuid, for instance, is Ill Thinking son of Ill Thought.

xii

Baligant's brave and handsome son Malpramis offers us only, alas, an Ill Promise. The infidel Abisme must surely represent the abyss, the pit of hell, and it is no coincidence that it is the archbishop, holy church, who overthrows him. The meaning of the name of the emperor's sword, Joyeuse, is stressed in the text, and may be linked with the joy pilgrims felt on first beholding Jerusalem; see laisses 183, 227 and notes. In despicable imitation Baligant names his sword Precious and makes that word the heathen warcry. Turpin's sword is called Almace, which scholars derive from an Arabic word meaning 'diamond' - perhaps like his horse he captured it from an enemy - and the name of Durendal, Roland's blazing weapon, not dimmed by the strongest sunshine, may derive from an Arabic word meaning 'shining, brilliant'. Other derivations, however, are also suggested. Roland's charger Veillantif translates as Wideawake, Ganelon's Tachebrun is Brown Patch, Marsile's Gaignun is Watchdog, Passecerf would outrun a deer and Saut Perdu is Lost Leap.

The names of the enemy's second and third gods remain obscure. Apollin carries echoes both of the Apollo of classical antiquity and of Apollyon, 'the angel of the abyss whose name is destruction' of Revelations ix 11. Ingenious attempts have been made to link the name Tervagant with ancient Germanic deities. Sadly diminished, this demon lingers in modern English as a scolding woman, a termagant.

Much speculation has been expended on the names of places and of heathen peoples. Readers who want to go more deeply into this can turn to Boissonnade's *Du nouveau sur la Chanson de Roland* which contains detailed and convincing arguments for trusting the *Roland* author and keeping the place names as he gives them. Editors do sometimes like to tidy names up into forms they find appropriate, rather than accepting them and dealing with them as they are. Boissonnade, however, considers that the *Roland* author knew what he was talking about, that while we cannot always respond to his references, his contemporaries certainly could, and that the place names and descriptions of territories in the poem refer to precise locations in Asia Minor, the Middle East, north Africa and above all in north eastern Spain, to the Ebro valley and plain and surrounding hills. I follow him therefore in retaining the manuscript's spelling of, for instance, Cordres, which he identifies with the town of Cortes on the Ebro downriver from Tudela. After capture by French forces this became, in fact not fiction, part of the fief of Rotrou du Perche of Normandy. There is no need to rename the town 'Cordoba' and then to accuse the author of stupidity in making his armies toil over impossibly long journeys from that distant southern stronghold. On the contrary, it is all quite local and all hangs together, if one does but trust the author. Boissonnade gives a host of similar examples.

In the same way the long enumeration of the forces composing Baligant's huge army includes an array of names which mean little to us but which must have reflected the experiences of crusaders in the Near and Middle East. Some we can identify: the Petchenegs, for instance, of laisse 239 were troops of Turkish race serving the emperor of Constantinople, who had occasion to use them more than once against undisciplined crusaders. Butentrot in laisse 236 may well be the name of a fearful pass in the Taurus mountains. The Armenians, laisse 237, were by no means always friendly to invading fellow-Christians. Canaanites, Hungarians, Bulgars and the terrifying black warriors of laisses 143 and 144 all reflect crusading realities. So do Baligant's Syrian scouts. The Huns, Avars and Sorbs, it is suggested, are a recollection of eighth century campaigns of Charlemagne.

Spellings of some of the personal names vary in different parts of the manuscript, Corsalis, for example, reappearing later as Corsablix, and Queen Bramimunde as Bramidonie. I have adopted one form and kept to it, following Bédier in calling the queen Bramimonde.

## SELECT BIBLIOGRAPHY

Photographic reproductions of Bodley's ms. Digby 23 include that by Samaran and Laborde, Paris (SATF).

### EDITIONS OF THE TEXT

These are many. Still invaluable is that of Joseph Bédier, text and modern French translation on facing pages, *La Chanson de Roland*, Paris 1921 and 1937.
Useful and easily available is F.Whitehead's *La Chanson de Roland*, Blackwell 1940 and later revisions; this has a good bibliography.
An admirable edition with commentary in Italian is that by Cesare Segre, Milan 1971.
The edition with facing translation by Gerard Moignet (Bibliothèque Bordas 1969) is well worth consulting.
So too is the thorough two-volume edition, with translation and commentary, *Song of Roland*, by Gerard J.Brault, Pennsylvania University Press 1978.

### OTHER WORKS

J.J.Duggan's *Guide to studies on the Chanson de Roland* is clear, helpful and easy to use. It surveys *Roland* studies briefly up to 1955 and treats those between that year and 1974 in greater detail. Grant and Cutler 1976.

The very many commentaries include:
Joseph Bédier, *La Chanson de Roland commentée*, Paris 1927 and 1968.
Edmond Faral, *La Chanson de Roland, étude et analyse*, Paris 1934.
Pierre Le Gentil, *La Chanson de Roland*, Paris 1955 1967; published in English, Harvard University Press 1969.

On place names and much else, see Prosper Boissonnade, *Du nouveau sur la Chanson de Roland*, Paris 1923, but see also the other place names studies listed in Duggan.

On the poem's distorted picture of Islam, see Sir Richard Southern, *Western Views of Islam in the Middle Ages*, Harvard University Press, 1962.

On the early history of Spain, see
J.B.Trend, *The Language and History of Spain*, London 1953, and Roger Collins, *Early Medieval Spain*, Macmillan 1983.

Of the many dictionaries used,
Randle Cotgrave, *A Dictionarie of the French and English Tongues*, London 1611, (half-size facsimile edition University of South Carolina Press 1968) has a value all its own.


Sincere thanks are due and are most warmly paid to Ann Gwilt, Mary and Chris Irwin, Vivien McKay, Pauline Matarasso, David Shirley and Susan Wicks for the help they have given me. This book is dedicated with gratitude and affection to the memory of Rhoda Sutherland.

# SONG OF ROLAND

*The poet announces his topic and sets the scene:*

## Laisse 1

Charlemagne the king, our emperor great Charles,
seven long years ago came here to Spain
and conquered it, conquered its lofty lands
to the far distant sea.  No city walls
need to be broken down, no castles stand
against our emperor - except one place:
obstinate Saragossa on its hill,
where King Marsile defies great Charlemagne.
Marsile does not love God.  To Apollin
he bows in prayer and to Mahomet turns.
Try as he may, evil will reach him there.

aoi

*At the Moslem king's court:*

## 2

Cool on a marble terrace, King Marsile
sat in his gardens under shady trees
among some twenty thousand of his knights.
From these he called to him his dukes and counts.
'Final disaster faces us,' he said.
'Great Charles the king and emperor of sweet France
has come into our land to conquer us.
I have no forces which can meet his host,
no numbers strong enough to break his charge.
You are my counsellors - advise me now!
Save me from death and shame.' But no one spoke.
None of the heathen had a word to say -
except for Blancandrin, Deep Valley's lord.

One of the wisest of the infidels
was Blancandrin, and a good fighting man,
able to serve his lord with hand or head.
'No need to be afraid,' he told the king.
'Send to proud Charles, send loving messages,
offer him faithful service, generous gifts:
hounds, lions, bears, a thousand moulted hawks,
seven hundred camels and four hundred mules
laden with gold and silver; fifty carts,
which he can drive away and use the gold
to pay his soldiers with. And tell the king
he's been in Spain too long. He should go home,
go home to Aix in France, and you yourself,
tell him, will join him there at Michaelmas*.
Tell him you'll then accept the Christian faith,
will do him loving homage, be his man.
If he wants hostages, then send him some.
He can have ten or twenty, that will do
to make him trust us. We can send the sons
our wives have given us. For life or death,
mine shall be one of them. Better by far
for them to die beheaded than for us
to lose all power and have to beg our bread.'

aoi

'And then,' said Blancandrin, 'the Franks will go.
By my right hand, by my long beard I swear,
they will break camp and go. They will disperse,
each lord to his own fief, the Franks to France,

for that's their homeland, and Charlemagne to Aix,
his royal chapel. There at Michaelmas
he'll hold high festival and wait for us.
The appointed day will come - and we shall not.
King Charles will wait it out and all day long
see not a sign of us. Cruel at heart,
a harsh and savage man, he'll kill the boys.
Our sons will die - yes, terrible. But worse
for us to lose fair Spain and suffer want!'
'Yes, he is right,' agreed the heathen lords.

5

Marsile dismissed the meeting. Then he called
ten of the worst of all his infidels:
Clarin of Balaguer, Estamarin,
his comrade Eudropin, and with these three,
long-bearded Guarlan, Priam, Machiner,
his uncle Maheu and from overseas
Malbien - Ill Good - and Jouner. Tenth and last
came white-haired Blancandrin, and he was named
to be their spokesman.
                        'Go, my noble lords,'
said King Marsile, 'and find the emperor.
He's at the town of Cordres, at the siege.
Take olive branches with you, let him see
you come in peace and true humility.
Use all your skill and make me this accord;
you shall have lands and fiefs,silver and gold,
as much as you can wish for.' But they said,
'We are already rich in all these things.'

aoi

## 6

The king dismissed his envoys:

                         'Go, my lords,
Take olive branches with you. Beg great Charles
in his God's name for mercy. Not one month
shall he see pass before I'll come to him
and bring a thousand vassals. I'll accept
the Christian faith and will become his man
in truth and love. If he wants hostages,
he certainly shall have them.'

                    'This will give
an excellent result,' said Blancandrin.

                                             aoi

## 7

Ten matching pure white mules were now led out:
golden the reins, the saddles silvered; all
a present from the king of Suatilie
to Saracen Marsile. They mount and ride.
Green olive branches in their hands, they come
to Cordres and to Charles, the lord of France.
Do what he will, he'll find himself deceived.

                                           aoi

*At Charlemagne's headquarters:*

## 8

At Cordres in a garden Charles the king
sits on a golden throne and laughs for joy.
Cordres has fallen. All its walls are smashed,
its towers toppled by his mangonels.
His knights are rich with plunder - silver, gold,

and valuable armour. In the town
there's not a heathen left - every last one
is either killed or christened. Charlemagne
sits in a spacious garden. Roland's there,
with Oliver, Duke Samson, Anséis,
and Geoffrey of Anjou, who has the right
to bear the royal standard. Gerier
is there with Gerin. So are many more,
some fifteen thousand Frenchmen from sweet France.
The older and the wiser sit on rugs
made of white silk and play at chess or tables.
The younger knights, light-footed, active men,
skirmish and practise swordplay with their friends.
Under a pine tree near an eglantine
is set a golden faldstool. On it sits
Charlemagne the emperor and lord of France.
White is his beard, snow-white his royal head,
his stature noble and his bearing proud.
No one who's seeking him needs to be told,
'Look, that's the king!'
    The messengers dismount
and greet the emperor with loving words.

*The Moslems offer terms:*

9

Lord Blancandrin spoke first, and said to Charles:
'The God of glory whom we must adore
preserve and prosper you! Marsile the king
has made close study of salvation's law;
and he intends to offer you a share,
a large share, of his riches - lions, bears,

fine hounds in leash, a thousand moulted hawks,
seven hundred camels and four hundred mules
laden with gold and silver; and with these
some fifty loaded wagons. Thus you'll have
as many golden bezants as you need,
and more besides, to pay your soldiers with.
You've stayed in Spain too long. You should go home.
Go home to France, to Aix, and there my lord
will come and join you. These are his very words.'
Charles raised his hands to heaven, bent his head
and set himself to ponder and reflect.

aoi

10

Head bent, the king sat thinking. All his life
Charlemagne was slow to speak, took time for thought.
Now when he raised his head, his look was grim.
'You gave your message well,' he said to them.
'Marsile your master is my enemy.
These offers that you make, to what extent
can they be guaranteed?'
                'Fully, my lord.
We offer hostages,' said Blancandrin.
'Ten or fifteen or twenty. My own son,
be it for life or death, shall go with them.
And there'll be others far more nobly born.
Then when you keep high feast at Michaelmas
in your great royal palace there at Aix,
my lord will come and join you. In the baths
God caused to spring there for you, he'll receive
the faith of Christ. These are the king's own words.'
'God can still save him,' said the emperor.      aoi

Westward the evening sun shone low and clear.
Charles had the ten mules stabled, and a tent
pitched in the gardens for the messengers.
Twelve servants cared for them attentively
and there all night they slept till daylight dawned.
The emperor heard matins and then mass.
Under a pine tree now he calls his lords
and they discuss what answer he should give.
The Franks of France shall guide him; no one else.

aoi

*The French discuss the offer:*

12

Charles sat beneath a pine and called his lords:
Ogier of Denmark; Turpin, who was Rheims'
holy archbishop; Richard, the old duke
of Normandy, who brought with him the boy,
his nephew Henry; noble Acelin,
the count of Gascony, a valiant man;
Theobald of Rheims and Milo, his close kin;
Gerin and Gerier; and with these came
Count Roland and his comrade Oliver,
the brave and noble knight. A thousand Franks
came at the emperor's word. And Ganelon,
the man who then betrayed them, he was there.
Discussions open; wickedness takes hold.

aoi

'My barons,' said the emperor, 'King Marsile
sends me an offer of enormous wealth -
hounds, lions, bears, a thousand moulted hawks,
seven hundred camels and four hundred mules
all bearing purest gold from Araby,
and fifty cartloads too. But he declares
I should go back to France, says he will come,
receive our holy faith and be baptised,
will do me homage and hold all his lands
in fief from me. But what he really wants
I do not know.'

            'This needs great care,' they said.

                                             aoi

14

The emperor had said his say. Roland sprang up
and spoke against the plan:

                      'Don't trust Marsile!
That is disastrous. Now it's seven years
since first we came to Spain. Neapolis
I've conquered for you, and Commibles as well,
and Balaguer, Bleak Valley, Tudela,
Pine with its lands and Sezilie - all these
I've won on your behalf. And King Marsile -
think what that traitor did at Sezilie!
He sent his fifteen infidels to you
with olive branches and fine promises,
just as he's doing now. You asked your Franks
what course they recommended. They advised
a piece of sheer stupidity, and you

did that same stupid thing. You sent our friends,
Basil and Basan, brothers, two of them,
to see the heathen king. There in the hills
under high Haltilie he took their heads.
Finish this war you started! Lead your host
to Saragossa, set the siege and stay,
stay all your life, if need be. Take revenge
on that foul murdering heathen for our friends!'

aoi

## 15

Head bent, the king sat silent, stroked his beard
and tugged at his moustache. He said no word,
praise or rebuke, to Roland. All the Franks
kept very quiet. Only Ganelon
rose and came forward, spoke with vehemence:
'Disastrous, yes, my lord, to trust a fool,
myself or any other, whose advice
conflicts with your advantage. King Marsile
offers joined hands and homage, wants to hold
the realm of Spain from you, wants to accept
the holy Christian faith. A man who says
we should reject this offer does not care
what sort of death we die. It is not right
for arrogance to rule. We should ignore
the words of fools and listen to the wise.'

aoi

## 16

Valiant Duke Naimon, held in more esteem
than any in the court, rose to his feet.
'You heard Count Ganelon, my lord,' he said.

'Considered properly, his words make sense.
Marsile has lost this war, he has no hope.
His fortresses are yours, his walls thrown down,
his cities burned and all his vassals crushed.
He's asking you for mercy; and it's wrong
to strike at him again. And don't forget,
he offers hostages. That being so,
we ought not now prolong this lengthy war.'
'The duke has spoken well,' agreed the Franks.

### 17

'My valiant lords,'said Charles,'whom shall we send
to Saragossa to the heathen king?'
'Send me,' Duke Naimon answered. 'Here I am,
give me the glove and staff.'
                              'No, by my beard!
You are intelligent, I need you here.
Go and sit down, no one's suggesting you.'

### 18

'My lords, my barons, whom do you suggest?
Who'll go and parley with the infidel?'
'I am the man to do it,' Roland said.
'Indeed you're not!' said Oliver his friend.
'You're far too proud, too savage, and I know
you'd go and pick a quarrel. If he likes,
the king can let me go.'
                         'Be quiet!' said Charles.
'Neither of you will stir a step from here.
And by my long white beard, I tell you all:
none of the Twelve Peers go. Be sure of that!'
The Franks fall silent, no one says a word.

Turpin of Rheims stood up and left his place.
'Let your Franks have some rest,' he said to Charles.
'Seven long years ago you brought them here;
think how they have toiled and suffered! Let me go.
Give me the glove and staff, and I'll find out
the truth about this Spaniard, if I can.'
'Back to your rug, sit down!' said the angry king.
'Keep your mouth shut unless I call on you.'

aoi

*Count Ganelon is chosen:*

20

'Come now, my knights, free Franks!' said Charlemagne.
'Choose me a lord from my own lands to take
my message to Marsile!' And Roland said,
'It shall be Ganelon, my stepfather.'
'Yes,' said the Franks, 'that's it! You cannot send
a cleverer man than that.'
                But Ganelon
was filled with rage and anger. Off he flung
his heavy mantle rich with marten fur
and stood resplendent there before them all
stripped to his silken tunic. Grey-eyed, proud,
tall and deep-chested, handsome, nobly built,
he was so glorious to look upon
that all his fellows gazed and gazed again.
'You crazy fool!' he said. 'Have you gone mad?
You are my stepson, don't they all know that?
And yet it's you who send me to Marsile!

Oh, if almighty God lets me come back
I shall do you such harm, such injury
that you will feel it to your dying day!'
'Folly and arrogance!' the count replied.
'Don't they all know I'm not afraid of threats?
But now this embassy - that needs good sense.
I'll do it for you, if the king permits.'

### 21

'For me you will do nothing!' he replied.
'I'm not your lord and you're no man of mine.
I serve the king. At his command I'll go
to Saragossa to the infidel.
But I shall find a way to make you feel
the full weight of my anger!' At these words,
Roland threw back his head and laughed aloud.

aoi

### 22

When he saw Roland laughing, Ganelon
felt he must crack with fury, split apart
or lose his senses. But instead he spoke:
'I count you worthless! You're the man who's forced
this wrongful choice on me.' To Charles he said,
'Just emperor, I'm quite ready and will go.

### 23

I understand that I must mount and ride                 aoi
for Saragossa, whence no man returns.
But listen first: your sister is my wife.
By her I have a son, the finest boy

of any in the world. Baldwin's his name,
and when he's grown he'll be a valiant knight.
My honours and my fiefs I leave to him.
I'll never see the boy. Protect him, king!'
'You feel too deeply,' said the emperor.
'My word is spoken, you will have to go.'

### 24

'Come forward, Ganelon,' said Charlemagne.
'Receive the glove and staff. You heard the Franks,
you know it's you they've chosen.'
                              'Yes,' he said.
'Roland has seen to that! I am his foe
until the day I die; and Oliver's,
because those two are comrades; and the Peers',
because they all love Roland. Witness, king:
here in your presence I defy them all.'
'No need,' said Charlemagne, 'for all this rage.
My order is given, you can only go.'
'Go, yes indeed, my lord. And how come back?
As safe as Basan and his brother did?'

aoi

### 25

The king held out his righthand glove. The count,
longing to be in any other place,
went to take hold of it, and down it fell.
There on the ground it lay.
                              'God,' cried the Franks,
'what dreadful loss must we expect from this?'
'That you'll find out, my lords,' said Ganelon.

'My lord,' he said, 'now give me leave to go.
As I've no choice, then let it be at once.'
'In Jesus' name and in my own,' said Charles,
'I give you blessing.' Raising his right hand,
he signed him with the cross, absolved his sins,
then handed him the letter and the staff.

*Ganelon's knights grieve for him:*

27

Back to his quarters went Count Ganelon
and there he dressed in his most splendid clothes,
hung Murglys at his side, buckled gold spurs
onto his heels, and mounted Tachebrun,
Brown Patch, his warhorse. Old Lord Guinemer,
Ganelon's uncle, held the stirrup firm.
How his knights grieved! In tears they crowded round,
cried out,
       'Alas for all your bravery!
Alas for your long service in the court,
noble and valiant heart, honoured by all!
No one, not even Charlemagne himself,
shall dare defend the man who forced on you
this dreadful task. Count Roland had no right
to make such a suggestion, for you come
of a most noble house.' And then they begged,
'My lord, let us come with you!'
                  'God forbid!'
he said to them. 'Better I die alone,
than take so many brave knights to their death.

Go home, my lords, home to sweet France, and greet
my wife there in my name, greet Pinabel,
my friend and fellow; greet my son as well,
Baldwin. You know the child. Give him your aid
and hold him for your lord.' So he set off
to go and see the heathen king, Marsile.

aoi

*The Christian and the Moslem reach an agreement:*

## 28

Under tall olive trees rode Ganelon
till he caught up the envoys. One of these,
Lord Blancandrin, reined back to meet the Frank.
Then side by side these clever men conversed -
'Charles,' said the heathen, 'is remarkable.
He overran Apulia and took
Calabria captive; then he crossed the sea
as far as England, where he forced them all
to pay St Peter's Pence*. Here in our land,
what does he want of us? Why has he come?'
'Such is his noble nature,' said the count.
'Now and forever, he's beyond compare.'

aoi

## 29

'How noble are the Franks!' said Blancandrin.
'But all those dukes and counts who give their lord
such bad advice, they do great harm to him,
as well as to other men.'
                         'I cannot think
of any man like that,' said Ganelon,

'unless you mean Count Roland. He indeed
must one day stumble. Only yesterday
our lord the king was sitting in the shade
during the morning - and up came the count,
still in his hauberk, only just returned
from laying waste the lands round Carcassonne.
He had a bright red apple in his hand.
'Fair uncle, here you are,' he said to Charles.
'A gift for you - the crown of every king
in all the world!' Such arrogance as this
must surely bring him down. Day in, day out,
in reckless pride he puts his life at risk.
If he were killed, then we could end this war.'

aoi

## 30

'He is quite ruthless, yes,' said Blancandrin.
'He wants to make all nations bow to him,
lays claim to every land. But tell me, how
does he intend to do this? On what men
does he rely for help?'
                              'Upon the Franks.
The men of France adore him, they will do
whatever he may ask. Silver and gold,
silks, armour, horses, mules, all these and more
he lavishes upon them. Why, the king,
great Charlemagne the emperor himself,
need lack for nothing. Any lands he wants
between here and the furthest Orient
Roland will conquer for his uncle's sake.'

aoi

*They come to Saragossa and King Marsile:*

31

So they ride on and so they talk, until
they come to an agreement: Roland dies.
This they confirmed on oath.
                              And on they rode
by paths and tracks until they could dismount
in Saragossa in a yew tree's shade.
There stood a faldstool underneath a pine,
covered with silk from Alexandria,
and on it sat the king, the lord of Spain.
Close round came twenty thousand Saracens;
not one man spoke, but listened for the words
the messengers would utter. Hushed they stood,
as Blancandrin and Ganelon approached.

32

Blancandrin took the Frenchman by the hand
and led him to Marsile.
                         'Great Apollin,
blessed Mahomet save you!' he began.
'We took your words to Charles. Lifting his hands,
he praised his god, but made us no reply.
He sends you here one of his greatest lords,
a man from France itself, powerful and rich.
From him you'll have your answer, war or peace.'
'Let the man speak, we'll hear him,' said Marsile.

aoi

*Ganelon deliberately enrages Marsile:*

### 33

But Ganelon had thought out with great care
what he was going to say. A cunning man,
skilled in the use of language, he began:
'The God of glory, whom we must adore,
preserve and keep you! Noble Charlemagne
sends me to tell you this: you shall accept
the holy Christian faith, and if you do,
King Charles will let you have one half of Spain
to hold from him in fief. If you refuse,
you will be taken, bound and carried off
by force to Aix for trial, judgment, death -
a vile and shameful death.' Appalled, the king
struck fiercely with a golden-feathered dart
at Ganelon, and would have wounded him
but for his lords, who caught and held the blow.                    aoi

### 34

Marsile changed colour, shook his javelin
so violently the Frank reached for his sword,
drew it a handsbreadth from its sheath and said,
'How fair you are, how bright! How many years
in the king's court I've worn you! Charles shan't say
that in a foreign land I died alone,
not till the best of them have paid for you!'
'Keep them apart!' exclaimed the Saracens.

### 35

Urged by his lords, the king sat down again.
'It's us you injure,' said the al-caliph,

'trying to strike the Frank! What you must do
is listen to the man, hear what he says.'
'This I must bear with patience,'said the count.
'Not all God's gold nor all the wealth of Spain
can stop me telling you - give me but time! -
what mighty Charlemagne sends me to say
to you, his mortal foe.' He flung aside
his silk and sable cloak - Lord Blancandrin
picked it up off the ground - but kept good hold
of Murglys' golden pommel, gripping it
ready in his right hand. The infidels,
gazing in wonder, said, 'A noble lord!'

aoi

*Again, Ganelon offers terms of peace which Marsile cannot accept:*

## 36

The count came nearer to the king again.
'You do wrong to be angry, King Marsile,'
he said to him. 'Great Charlemagne, my lord,
sends me to tell you this: if you accept
the holy Christian faith, then he will grant
one half of Spain to you to hold in fief.
Roland, his sister's son, will hold the rest.
An arrogant co-tenant you will have!
Refuse this, and my lord sets siege to you
in Saragossa, has you taken, bound,
and carried off to Aix - not on a mule,
hack, palfrey, warhorse, nothing you can ride,
but trussed and thrown on some pack animal.
Once there and tried, your head will be cut off.
Here is the letter from our emperor.'
He put the letter in Marsile's right hand.

*Charlemagne's letter is quite different:*

37

The king was white with rage. He broke the seal,
threw down the wax and read the letter.
                                        'Charles,
lord of France, here tells me to recall
the grief I caused, the anger that they feel,
for Basil and his brother, those two counts
whose heads I cut off in high Haltilie.
If I would save my life, then I must send
my uncle to his court, the al-caliph.
If I will not, then there can be no peace.'
'Then Ganelon spoke nonsense!' said the prince,
young Jurfaret. 'He's far out of his brief,
he should not live. Father, give him to me,
I will do justice on him.' Ganelon
brandished his sword, sprang to the pine tree's trunk
and set his back against it, facing them.

*None the less, Marsile trusts Ganelon:*

38

Deeper into the gardens went Marsile,
taking his chief men with him. Jurfaret,
his only son and heir, and Marganice,
uncle, al-caliph, vassal to the king,
and old white-headed Blancandrin went too.
'My lord, send for the Frank,' said Blancandrin.
'He'll be of use to us; I have his word.'
'Then fetch him,' said the king. So Blancandrin
went back to Ganelon, took his right hand,

and led him through the gardens to the king.
And there they planned the treason they would do.

aoi

### 39

'Fair sir,' said King Marsile, 'I was quite wrong
to strike at you in anger as I did.
Accept this sable mantle as a pledge
of recompense. The gold on it alone
would fetch five hundred pounds. Tomorrow night
shall see it handsomely redeemed.'
                       'My lord,
indeed I don't refuse it,' said the count.
'May God in heaven reward you, if he will!'

aoi

### 40

'From henceforth, Ganelon,' said King Marsile,
'I shall be very much your friend. But now
I want to hear you talk of Charlemagne.
Your emperor is so old, his years are spent,
two hundred years and more, so people say.
Across how many countries has he fought,
how many blows has taken on his shield,
how many mighty kings compelled to go
and beg their bread! When will he tire of war?'
'His character forbids,' said Ganelon.
'No one who knows the king but will agree
that he's a fighting man. His worth outstrips
all words that I could find. Who could express
his mighty courage, his heroic strength?

Glorious his blazing valour, sent by God!
Valiant his glorious nobles - he would die
sooner than fail his men or let them down.'

41

'I find Charlemagne amazing,' said the king.
'An old, old man, white-haired, white-bearded, more,
so it's said, than two hundred years in age.
Think of his hard campaigns in foreign lands,
think of the wounds he's taken from sharp spears,
of the rich kings that he's brought down and forced
to turn to beggary! When will he tire
of so much war?'

              'Never, while Roland lives,'
said Ganelon. 'His like cannot be found
under the arch of heaven. Oliver,
his dearest comrade, he's a valiant man.
And the Twelve Peers on whom great Charles relies,
these lead his vanguard, twenty thousand knights.
Charlemagne is safe, he fears no man alive.'

                                      aoi

42

'I am astonished,' said the Saracen,
'at that white-haired old man. I'm told they say
that he has lived two hundred years and more.
Countless the distant countries he has won,
countless the thrusts given by keen-edged swords,
countless the mighty kings left lying dead
on many battlefields! When will he cease
to wish for war?'

'Not while his nephew lives,'
said Ganelon. 'There's no such warrior
between here and the East. How valiant too
is Oliver, his comrade! And the Twelve,
whom Charles so greatly values, they command
the Frankish vanguard, twenty thousand men.
Charles is afraid of no one, he is safe.'

aoi

### 43

'Fair my lord Ganelon,' said King Marsile,
'My people are the finest in the world
and can provide four hundred thousand knights.
Can I oppose Charles and his Franks with these?'
'Not at this time,' he answered. 'You would lose
too many of your heathen. No, avoid
such foolish action, use intelligence.
Send lavish gifts to Charles, amaze them all;
then, when you give him twenty hostages,
the king will go away, home to sweet France,
and leave behind his rearguard. In command
he'll place Count Roland and Count Oliver,
the brave and courteous, I'm quite sure of that.
Take my advice and they are both dead men.
Great Charles will see his pride come crashing down;
he'll never want to challenge you again.'

aoi

### 44

'And how can I make certain,' said Marsile,
'of Roland's death?'
                      'Oh, I can tell you that!

Wait till the king has reached the pass at Cize,'
Count Ganelon replied. 'He'll post his men,
Roland the mighty, faithful Oliver
and twenty thousand Franks, to guard his rear.
Against these launch your troops, a first assault,
one hundred thousand of your infidels!
They'll cut the Franks to pieces - your men too,
they'll suffer grievous loss, be sure of that.
Then you send in a second wave of troops
to make a fresh attack. In one or other,
Count Roland can't escape, must surely die.
You'll have achieved a noble feat of arms,
you'll have won peace to last you all your life!

aoi

### 45

If Roland can be killed, this will cut off
Charlemagne's right hand. Never again he'll raise
those massive armies, never summon more
those endless warring hosts. And the Great Land
will enjoy peace at last.' The heathen king
listened attentively, embraced the count,
and after that unlocked his treasury.

aoi

*Ganelon and Marsile both swear to procure Roland's death:*

### 46

'What need for more discussion?' said Marsile.
'But any plan is useless [till confirmed].
You will betray Count Roland. Swear it now!'
'As it shall please you,' answered Ganelon,

and on the relics housed in Murglys' hilt
he swore the treason and his own black shame.

aoi

### 47

There was a faldstool there of ivory.
Marsile sent for a book in which was written
the law of Mahomet and of Tervagant.
On this he swore that he and all his men
would find and kill Count Roland if they could.
'Good luck go with you!' answered Ganelon.

aoi

*The Moslem lords and the queen come forward in turn to greet
Ganelon:*

### 48

Now up came Valdabrun, a heathen lord,
godfather to Marsile. He gave the count
a brilliant smile and said,
                              'Here, take my sword,
No man on earth possesses one as good.
The hilt contains a thousand *manguns.** Now
I give it you, fair sir, in friendliness,
since you intend to help us, so that we
can find brave Roland on the battlefield.'
'Indeed I do,' he said, and so they kissed
like friends on face and chin.

### 49

Next came an infidel called Climorin,
and with a pleasant laugh he said,

'My lord,
accept my helmet. It's by far the best
I've ever seen. And you will help us bring
Roland the marquis to disgrace and shame.'
'Most certainly,' the count said, and the two
kissed on the mouth and face.

aoi

### 50

And then the queen came forward, Bramimonde.
'My lord and all his men, fair sir,' she said,
'hold you in high esteem, and so must I.
I send your wife two clasps, both rich with gold,
jacinths and emeralds. These are worth more
than all the wealth of Rome. Your emperor
never set eyes on better.' Ganelon
took the queen's gifts and put them in his pouch.

aoi

### 51

Marsile called to his treasurer, Malduit:
'The goods for Charles, are they all ready?'

'Yes,
ready, my lord,' he said. 'Silver and gold
on seven hundred camels; hostages,
twenty of these, all of the highest birth.'

aoi

*Marsile promises the traitor further riches:*

### 52

Gripping the Frenchman's shoulder, Marsile said,
'You are a clever and courageous man.

By all you hold most holy, I say this:
be sure you don't desert us. I shall send
enormous wealth to you, ten mules with gold
from Araby, and every year ten more
just as well laden shall be sent to you.
Take this great city's keys and offer them
with all the riches of the town to Charles.
Then set me Roland in the rearguard!
Let me but find him in the mountain pass
and I'll do battle with him to the death.'
'Soon, for the waiting hurts me!' said the count.
He mounted and began his journey back.                    aoi

*The scene shifts; Charlemagne and his knights are waiting for*
*Ganelon's return:*

### 53

Returning to his base, the emperor,
great Charlemagne, now lay encamped at Galne.
This was a city taken and laid waste
by Roland, who had done the work so well
no one could live there for a hundred years.
Here the king waits for news of Ganelon,
and for the tribute payments due to him
from the wide lands of Spain.
                              In early dawn
as day began to brighten, Ganelon
arrived at Galne and rode into the camp.

                                                    aoi

*Ganelon persuades the emperor that all is well and he can go back to France. The war is over:*

54

The king had risen early, he had heard
matins and mass already. Now he stood
on the green grass outside his tent. There too
were valiant Roland, courteous Oliver,
Duke Naimon, many more. Guilty, forsworn,
came clever Ganelon to join his peers.
And cleverly he spoke:

'God give you health!'

he said to Charlemagne. 'Here are the keys
of Saragossa. And I have arranged
for its enormous wealth to come to you,
and twenty hostages. Have them kept safe!
Besides this, King Marsile wants you to know
he would have sent the caliph if he could.
With my own eyes I saw him with his ships
putting to sea. Four hundred thousand knights
went with him in the ships, all fully armed,
girt with gold-pommelled swords richly inlaid,
helms closed and hauberks on. They left Marsile
and fled away, refusing to accept
the Christian faith. Not four leagues had they sailed
when storms swept down and drowned them, every one.
You will set eyes on none of them, I swear.
I would have brought the caliph, if he'd lived.
As for the king, you can trust me, my lord:
before the month is out, heathen Marsile
will follow you to France, will there accept
our holy Christian faith, will kneel to you

in homage, hands in yours, and will receive
his realm of Spain from you.'
                              'Thanks be to God!'
said Charlemagne. 'Count, you have done this well.
You shall be much the richer for your work.'
A thousand bugles blow. The French break camp,
have their beasts loaded and set off for France.

aoi

*The French army sets off for home:*

## 55

Great Charles the emperor has ravaged Spain,
captured her castles, laid her cities waste.
His war, he says, is done.  He rides for France.
Day passes and now night begins to fall.
High on a hill top Roland plants his spear;
his banner flies from it, and all around
the French encamp. Their spreading numbers fill
the upland valleys and the country round.
And through these lofty valleys heathen ride,
helmets and hauberks on, shields at their necks,
swords girded, lances ready. Now they halt.
In woods high up among the peaks they wait;
four hundred thousand of them wait for dawn.
Ah God, how sad it is the French don't know!

aoi

*Encamped, the sleeping emperor dreams:*

## 56

Day passes, dark night falls, the emperor sleeps.
And as he slept, he dreamed and thought he gripped
his ashen-hafted spear firm in both hands

in the high pass at Cize. Count Ganelon
in fury, raging, wrenched it from his grasp,
brandished and broke it till the splinters flew
up to the sky. The emperor did not wake.

### 57

Another vision came to him in dream:
he was in France, at Aix, in his own chapel -
a vicious boar gripped him by the right arm
and sank its fangs into his very flesh.
He saw a leopard charge from the Ardennes;
this too attacked him savagely. And then
from deep in his own hall came racing up
a greyhound, leaping, bounding, and tore off
the boar's right ear, then furiously attacked
the raging leopard. All the watching French
exclaimed at the encounter and they asked
which of the beasts would win. But Charlemagne
still slept and lay unstirring on his bed.

aoi

*Day time, and the French must appoint a rearguard before the main army crosses the Pyrenees; Ganelon names his stepson to command it:*

### 58

Night passed and bright day broke. Shrill trumpets rang
resounding through the host. Proudly the king
rode out before his men.
           'My barons, look!
There are the passes and the narrow ways
ahead of us,' he said. 'Choose me the man

who shall command the rearguard.' Instantly:
'Roland, my stepson,' Ganelon replied,
'most valiant of your lords.' Fierce was the look
the king turned on him when he heard those words.
'Devil in human shape!' he said to him.
'Some fatal madness drives you. But then who
shall lead my vanguard, go ahead of us?'
'Ogier the Dane,' he answered. 'There's not one
among your lords more fitted for the task.'

59

Hearing his own name chosen, Roland spoke          aoi
as a knight should:
                    'I owe you thanks, my lord,
sir stepfather! You choose me to command
the emperor's rearguard - be assured of this:
he shall not lose one palfrey, charger, mule,
jennet, pack animal or saddle horse
that is not taken from me by the sword.'
'Indeed, I am sure of it,' said Ganelon.

                                              aoi

60

And in a fury Roland said to him,
'Son of a serf! You evil stinking wretch,
did you suppose I'd drop the emperor's glove,
the way you dropped the staff he'd given you?'

                                              aoi

61

'Just emperor,' said Roland to the king,
'give me the bow you have there. None will say

it slipped out of my hand - unlike the staff
you gave to Ganelon!' Charles bent his head,
fingered his beard and tugged at his moustache.
In vain he struggled to hold back his tears.

62

Naimon came forward now, as fine a man
as any in the court.
                          'You heard it all,'
he said to Charlemagne, 'and you can see
how angry Roland is. He has been named;
none of your lords can alter that, it's done.
Give him that bow you bent, and then make sure
he has sufficient men, the best support.'
The king held out the bow, which Roland grasped.

63

'Be sure of this, fair nephew,' said the king:
'I shall leave half my forces here with you.
Take them, and you'll be safe.'
                          'Never!' he said.
'May God confound me if I so belie
our reputation! No, I'll keep with me
our twenty thousand valiant Franks, and you
shall cross the pass in safety. While I live,
no man on earth shall give you cause to fear.'

*Count Roland picks his men:*

64

Count Roland mounts his warhorse. To him came          aoi
his comrade Oliver to ride with him,

came Gerin with his brave friend Gerier,
came Otho, Berenger and Anséis
the fierce and proud, came Astor and the duke
great Gaifier, and the old man too, Gerard
of Roussillon. Turpin, the archbishop, cried,
'I'll go with Roland, on my life, I will!'
'And so will I,' said Walter, count of Hum.
'I'm his own man and cannot fail him now.'
And then they chose their twenty thousand knights.

aoi

### 65

Roland commanded Walter: 'Take with you
a thousand Franks from our own France and hold
the heights and narrow places. See that Charles
does not lose one man there.'                  aoi
　　　　　　　　　'My lord, for you
this is my simple duty,' said the count.
He took the men and led them to patrol
the peaks and narrow gorges. No bad news
will make him leave those heights or quit his post,
not until seven hundred swords are drawn.
Today King Almaris, lord of Belferne,
will offer battle and destroy them all.

*Charlemagne and his host ride through the high pass:*

### 66

High are the peaks and shadowy the depths,
dark the great rocks, the narrows perilous.
All day the Frankish host labours across

in pain and danger. Fifteen leagues away
their going can be heard.

            And now the French
reach the Great Land, see across Gascony,
their lord's domain; now their own fiefs and lands
come to their minds, as do their noble wives
and the young girls. Not one man there but weeps.
Charles is more moved than any. He has left
his nephew Roland in the gates of Spain.
Compassion grips the king and he must weep.

                                      aoi

## 67

All the Twelve Peers are left behind in Spain,
they and their twenty thousand Franks. No fear,
no dread of death disturbs them in the least.
On into France rides Charles, and hides his face
under his cloak. Duke Naimon, next to him,
asked him,

        'Why are you sad?'
             'You should not ask!'
said Charles. 'My grief's too great, I cannot feign.
France is to be destroyed by Ganelon.
Last night an angel showed me in a dream -
smashing my spear to pieces in my hands
was that same man who picked my sister's son,
Count Roland, to command the rear. Alas,
and I have left him in a hostile land!
God, if he's lost, I've none to take his place!'

                                      aoi

Charles cannot check his tears. Compassion moves
a hundred thousand Franks; they grieve for him
and greatly fear for Roland. Roland's sold.
Huge payment has vile Ganelon received -
silver and gold, silk fabrics, horses, mules,
lions and camels - from the heathen king.

*King Marsile gathers his troops:*

Now King Marsile has summoned all his men,
his lords of Spain. His counts and viscounts come,
with dukes, with emirs and with *almaçurs*
and *cunturs'* sons. Four hundred thousand men
within three days ride in to join the king.
In Saragossa now his drums speak loud*.
They set Mahomet on the highest tower,
no heathen there but bows down and adores.
They mount and ride, each striving to be first,
over the level ground*, up hill, down dale,
until they see the banners of the Franks.
The rearguard and the Twelve will not be slow
to offer battle to the heathen host.

*Marsile appoints his commanders, who make their boasts before the king:*

Now bright with laughter Aelroth rode out,
King Marsile's nephew, touching on his mule.
'Long have I worked for you, my lord,' he cried,
'laboured and toiled, great battles fought and won.
Reward me now: give me the right to strike

first blow at Roland. On my spear he dies!
Mahomet helping me, I'll free all Spain
from the high passes down to Durestant.
Charles will be weary, recreant his Franks.
You need fight no more wars in all your life!'
Granting this right, Marsile gave him his glove.

aoi

### 70

Aelroth grasped it, shouted with fierce pride,
'A noble gift, my lord! Now choose me twelve
among your barons. They and I will fight
against the Franks' Twelve Peers.' Immediately
King Marsile's brother, Falsaron, exclaimed,
'I shall go with you, nephew. You and I
will rule this fight together. Charlemagne
must lose the rearguard of his mighty host.
Their doom is spoken, we shall kill them all.'

aoi

### 71

Then up rode Corsalis, a Berber king,
skilled in all evil arts, and said his say
like a true vassal. Not for all God's gold
would this man do a deed of cowardice.
. . . . . . . . . . . . . . . . . . . . . . . . . . . . . .
Malprimis of Brigant spurred forward next -
a man who runs faster than any horse -
and cried out loud before his king Marsile,
'I'm going to Roncevaux! If Roland's there,
I shan't draw back from battle till he's dead!'

There was an emir there from Balaguer,
a man of noble build, with bright proud look.
Once armed and mounted, joyfully he rides,
and with such courage! What a valiant knight
he would have made, had he but been baptised!
'To Roncevaux!' he cried before Marsile.
'Roland is dead, if I can find him there.
And so is Oliver, so are the Peers,
all twelve of them. In sorrow and in shame
the French will die. King Charles is feeble, old,
too weak to fight. Spain will be ours and free!'
Gratefully King Marsile received his words.

aoi

Next came an *almaçur* from Moriane,
as vile a man as any in all Spain.
Before Marsile he made his boast:
                              'My lord,
I'll lead my company to Roncevaux,
all twenty thousand armed with shield and lance.
If I find Roland, death I promise him.
No day shall pass when Charlemagne does not weep!'

aoi

Turgis of Turtelosa rides out next.
He is a count; that town belongs to him.
He longs to slaughter Christians.
                              'Never fear!
Mahomet's much more powerful than their saint,

their Roman Peter!' Turgis cried. 'Serve him,
and we shall win the field. Now I shall go
and face Count Roland there in Roncevaux.
No one on earth can save him from my sword!
Look, see how long it is, how strong! You'll hear
which is the master, Durendal or mine!
If they dare face us, all the Franks will die.
Doting old Charles will suffer shame and grief,
he'll never wear his kingly crown again!'

75

Escremiz of Bleak Valley followed him.
He is a Saracen, lord of that fief.
Before Marsile among the throng he cried,
'I'm going to Roncevaux to bring down pride!
Let me find Roland, he won't take his head
home on his shoulders! Nor will Oliver,
who gives the rest their orders, nor those Peers.
Each one's condemned to death. The French will die,
Charles have no vassals, France have no men left!'

aoi

76

Two foul deceiving traitors were the next,
Estramariz and his friend Esturgant.
'Barons, come forward,' said Marsile. 'You two
shall help to lead my men at Roncevaux
in the high passes.'

        'Sir, at your command,'
the heathen answered. 'We will find and kill
Roland and Oliver and all Twelve Peers.

Sharp are our swords and strong; they shall be red
in hot French blood. Dead shall the Frenchmen lie,
their old king weep! To you, my lord, we'll give
the Great Land for your own. Come, you shall see,
we'll offer you the emperor himself!'

### 77

Next racing up came handsome Margariz,
lord from Seville to the far Cazmarines.
Women adore him for his looks. Not one
but laughs for joy, and smiles to welcome him;
they cannot help themselves. He's the best knight
of all the heathen chivalry. Now fast
he joins the throng and shouts above them all,
'Don't be afraid, my lord! In Roncevaux
I shall kill Roland. Oliver will die,
so will their dozen peers. Look at my sword
golden the hilt, it was a gift to me
from Primès' emir - red shall be the blade,
red with French blood I promise you, and dead
shall Frenchmen lie, France be disgraced, and Charles,
white-bearded dotard, not a day shall pass
but he shall rage and weep at his great loss!
Within a year we shall have France itself,
sleep if we want to in St Denis' town!'
Deeply the heathen king bowed him his thanks.

aoi

### 78

Next came Chernuble, lord of Munigre.
His hair trails on the ground and he can lift -
just for a joke, just to amuse himself -

a greater weight than four pack-mules can bear.
No sun shines in his land, so it is said,
no corn can grow, there is no rain, no dew,
and all the stones are black. Some people say
that devils live there. Now he made his boast:
'I've buckled on my sword. In Roncevaux
I'll go and dye it red. If Roland's there
and I can find him and do not attack,
then never trust me more! This sword of mine
shall beat down Durendal, the French shall die
and France remain bereft.' His speech was done.
The twelve companions gathered, and they led
a hundred thousand valiant Saracens,
hungry for war each one, into a wood,
where under pine trees they put on their arms.

*The Moslem host pursues the French:*

79

Of Saracenic work and triple strength,
the heathens' hauberks; Saragossan helms
of highest quality; their swords are made
of strong Viana steel; excellent spears
come from Valencia, and at their points
flutter the pennons, yellow, white and red.
Palfreys and mules they leave; now warhorses
the heathen mount; and closely ranked move off.
Clear was the morning sky and bright the sun;
no piece of armour there but blazed and shone
under its rays and gave its brilliance back.
A thousand trumpets woke more glory still.

Loud was their voice and shrill; it reached the Franks.
'Sir comrade,' said Count Oliver, 'I'm sure
we shall have battle soon.'
                              'God grant we may!'
Roland replied. 'We owe it to our king
to stand here for his sake. For his own lord
a man must bear all ills, he must endure
extremes of heat and cold, lose hair and hide.
Strike hard, each one of you! Let no one sing
foul songs about our fight! Heathen are wrong,
Christians are in the right. God fights for us.
Don't look to me to see how cowards act!'

aoi

*Count Oliver observes the enemy, and begs Roland to call the*
*emperor back:*

### 80

High on a peak stood Oliver and looked
into a grassy valley on his right,
far down below him, full of Saracens.
He saw the endless heathen hordes approach
and called to Roland:
                        'I can see the glint
of steel coming from Spain - hauberks and helms,
innumerable, glittering in the sun.
They'll cut our Franks to pieces. He knew this,
that traitor Ganelon, when he picked us
in the king's council!'
                        'Quiet!' Roland said.
'The man's my stepfather, don't speak of him.'

Up on a hill top Oliver looked out.
Clearly he saw the realm of Spain, saw too
the countless host of heathen, saw the sun
glitter on gold-rich helmets, shining shields,
on inlaid hauberks, spears and pennons bright.
The very squadrons were too numerous,
far more than he could count. In anxious haste
he hurried down the hill as best he could,
rejoined the Franks and told them what he had seen.

'I've seen the infidels!' said Oliver.
'No man alive has ever seen such hordes.
In the front rank a hundred thousand ride,
shields slung and helmets laced. So many spears
carried upright! So many hauberks gleam!
Soon now you'll have to fight as none have fought.
My lords of France, now draw your strength from God!
Stand in the field, stand firm, avoid defeat!'
'The devil take all cowards!' cry the Franks.
'None of us here will fail you, though we die.'

aoi

*Roland will not humble himself to call for help:*

'Their force is huge,' said Oliver, 'and ours
is far too small. Comrade, blow the great horn!
The king will hear it and bring back the host.'
'A stupid thing to do!' Roland replied.
'I'd lose all my renown at home in France.

Soon now I'll strike great blows with Durendal,
redden her blade from tip to golden hilt.
Their own ill luck brings these vile heathen here!
You have my word on it, they'll soon be dead.'

aoi

## 84

'Roland, I beg you, sound the oliphant!
Charlemagne will hear it and bring back his men,
he and the host will help us.'
                              'God forbid
that I should ever so disgrace my kin
or so dishonour France!' Count Roland said.
'How hard I'll hit with Durendal! You'll see
her sharp blade drip with blood. I promise you,
these heathen scum are riding to their death.'

aoi

## 85

'Roland, my comrade, sound your oliphant!
Charlemagne will hear it up there in the pass,
the Franks, I tell you, will come back at once.'
'Almighty God forbid that any man,'
Roland replied, 'should have the power to say
I blew for help against the infidels!
No kin of mine shall suffer that disgrace.
In the great battle soon you'll see me strike
a thousand blows and seven hundred more
and shining Durendal all red with blood.
Our Franks are valiant men, you'll see them fight!
No power on earth can save those infidels.'

'There's no disgrace!' said Oliver. 'I've seen
the Spanish Saracens. Valleys and hills,
the open spaces and the plains, they're full!
The heathen swarm in hordes, and we are few!'
'So much the better for us!' Roland said.
'God and his saints and angels all forbid
that I should shame sweet France! I'd rather die!
The emperor loves us for the blows we strike.'

Roland is valiant, Oliver is wise,
both are outstanding on the field of war.
Once armed and mounted, there's no thought of death
can hold them from the fight. Excellent men,
noble and proud their words!
                      Now faster still
the wicked heathen ride, the hordes draw near.
'Look at them, Roland!' said Count Oliver.
'How near they are, how far away the king!
You wouldn't condescend to blow the horn.
If Charles were here with us, we'd take no harm.
Look up towards the Gates of Spain and see
the miserable rearguard! All of them
face their last battle; these won't fight again.'
'Don't talk such rubbish!' Roland answered him.
'Be damned to coward hearts! We shall stand firm,
we'll hit out hard, we'll wound and kill them all!'

aoi

*The French prepare for battle:*

88

Fell as a lion or leopard, Roland now,
seeing the battle near, called up fierce rage,
cried to the Franks, shouted to Oliver:
'Comrade, dear friend, don't say that! It was Charles
who picked these men, all twenty thousand knights!
Well does he know there's not a coward here!
For his lord's sake a man must bear great ills,
endure fierce heat and bitter cold, must lose
both blood and flesh. Use your lance well, hit hard,
as I'll use Durendal, the king's own gift.
And if I die, the man who has her next
can say it was a fighter owned her once!'

89

Turpin the archbishop spurred, rode up a slope,
and there addressed the Franks:
                              'My noble lords,
Charles placed us here! We owe it to our king
to die for him. Fight now for Christendom!
You can all see the Saracens, you know
how near the battle is. Confess your sins,
ask God for mercy. I'll absolve you all,
to save your souls. And if you die you'll sit
enthroned as martyrs in high paradise.'
The Franks dismounted, knelt, and in God's name
Turpin absolved and blessed them, ordering them
in penance for their sins to strike out hard.

The French rose to their feet, absolved and clean,
in God's name blessed by Turpin. Now they mount
their fretting coursers, each man well prepared,
as a knight should be, ready for the fight.
'Comrade, you were quite right,' Count Roland said.
'Coined money, wealth and gold that man has had.
Count Ganelon has sold us. Charlemagne
will certainly take vengeance. And for now,
although Marsile has bought us, he'll soon find
his bargain's not complete, he'll need his sword!'

aoi

Out from the Gates of Spain Count Roland rides
on his swift charger Wideawake. How well
his shining arms become him! As he goes,
he lets his heavy spear spin in his hand
and twirls the gleaming point up to the sky.
White flies the pennon from its tip and gold
the streamers fall and brush against his hands.
His face is bright with laughter and his form
noble indeed. His comrade follows him,
and all the Franks shout out to greet the count,
their strong defender. Fiercely now he looks
towards the Saracens, and humbly then,
with kindness at the Franks. To these he says,
courteous and gentle,
                      'Soft, my lords, walk on!
These infidels are coming to be killed.
What plunder we shall win, how rich and rare,

better than kings of France have ever won!'
Less and less grows the space between the hosts.

aoi

### 92

'I have no heart for words,' said Oliver.
'You would not stoop to blow the oliphant,
you've no support from Charles, he doesn't know
what's happening here, no fault of his. Nor theirs,
those men there in the field, no blame to them!
Now ride, my noble lords, ride on and charge!
Stand firm, I beg you! For God's sake resolve
to give and take hard blows! And don't forget
the emperor's battle-cry!' At this the Franks
cried out, 'Mountjoy!'* Any who heard that sound,
with what heroic thoughts their minds would fill!
And now they ride, ah God, how fierce they ride,
spurring their horses to go faster yet!
So they charge home. What else is there to do?
Nor are the Saracens at all afraid.
The Frankish and the heathen forces meet.

aoi

*Battle is joined; single encounters:*

### 93

Out in the front, ahead of all the rest,
rode Aelroth, Marsile's nephew. As he went,
he shouted insults at our Frankish knights:
'Today, you filthy Frenchmen, joust with us!
Your own liege lord has sold you! Charles was mad
to leave you in the pass here. Now sweet France

will lose her glory, and your emperor Charles
the right hand from his body!' Hearing this,
ah God, how Roland raged! He spurred, rode hard
and struck with all his force. Clean through the shield
he drove, through hauberk, breastbone, flesh,
smashing the bones, cutting the backbone free.
With his great spear the heathen's soul he hurled
out of his body. Thus transfixing him,
he shook him on his spear and tossed him dead,
snapping his neck in two. Then not content,
he spoke to his dead foe:
                            'Son of a slave!
Charles is not mad, never loved treachery,
did right to place us here to guard the pass.
No glory does sweet France lose here today.
Strike at them, Franks, the first encounter's ours!
We're in the right, these heathen scum are wrong!'

                                                    aoi


### 94

A duke was there, his name was Falsaron,
King Marsile's brother, lord of all the land
from Balbiun to Atliun*. Under the sky
there's none more criminal. Between his eyes
the span's enormous, six-inch at the least.
Great was his grief to see his nephew killed.
He spurred out from the throng, shouting the cry
so loathsome to the Franks:
                            'Today sweet France
loses her honour!' Oliver heard this
and in great anger drove his golden spurs

into his horse's sides and rode full tilt
against the heathen duke. Through shield and mail
and deep into his flesh he sank the lance,
pennon and all. He tossed him to the ground,
then looking at the wretch who lay there dead,
fiercely exclaimed,

                'Your threats don't trouble me,
you slave-born scum! Strike at them Franks, strike hard!
We can soon finish these!' And then, 'Mountjoy!'
he shouts, 'Mountjoy!', great Charles' battle-cry.

                                              aoi

95

And there's a king there too called Corsalis,
a Berber from a foreign land, who shouts
to tell his fellow-infidels, 'These men
will be no trouble, look how few there are!
A worthless handful! Great Charlemagne will save
not one of them. This is the day they die!'
Archbishop Turpin heard him; hated him;
drove deep his golden spurs and with great strength
charged home. He shattered the shield and hauberk,
rammed his great spear right through him, then he shook
the spitted corpse out from the saddlebows
and dropped it on the track. Now looking back
at the vile wretch, he shouted,

                        'Slave, you lied!
Daily the king my lord defends us all;
our Franks don't run away; and your men there,
we'll bring them to a halt! I've news for you:
today's the day you die! Frenchmen, hit hard!

Let none forget himself! The first blow's ours,
thanks be to God!' And then, to hold the field,
Archbishop Turpin shouted out, 'Mountjoy!'

### 96

And Gerin struck Malprimis of Brigal,
whose fine shield did no pennyworth of good.
The crystal boss was shattered, half the shield
spun right away, and Gerin drove his spear
through hauberk into flesh and thrust it home,
so that the heathen fell all at a blow.
Stone dead he dropped and Satan took his soul.

aoi

### 97

His comrade Gerier rode to attack
the heathen emir, shattered shield and mail,
set the spearpoint into his guts and forced
the whole head through his body, tossed it down.
'Excellent fighters, ours!' said Oliver,

### 98

Duke Samson chose the *almaçur*, rode hard,
drove steel through golden-flowered shield, through mail,
through liver, heart and lungs, and flung him dead
down on the ground, grieve or rejoice who may.
'A noble blow!' Archbishop Turpin said.

### 99

And at full gallop Anséis charged and met
Turgis of Turtelosa, broke his shield

under the golden boss, smashed through linked mail,
set his sharp point full in the heathen's flesh
and with a powerful thrust drove it right through
and out behind his back. With shaft outstretched,
he overthrew him dead onto the ground.
'A warrior's stroke, that one!' Count Roland said.

100

Now Engeler the Gascon of Bordeaux
spurred, slackened rein, and charged at Escremiz,
lord of Bleak Valley, smashed the heathen's shield
clear off his shoulder, shivered it to bits,
drove through the hauberk's throatpiece, struck the man
full in the chest under the collarbones.
Dead from his seat he hurled him, lance outstretched,
and yelled at him,
                    'You came here to be damned!'

aoi

101

Next Walter struck the heathen Esturgant
high on his shield, so that he cut right off
its red and white, then pierced the chainmail links,
drove his sharp spear into his flesh and flung
the infidel dead from his racing horse.
'No hope there now for you!' he jeered at him.

102

And Berenger attacked Astramariz,
broke through both shield and mail, sank his strong spear
into his flesh and tossed him dead among
a thousand Saracens. Of their twelve peers,

ten have been killed, now only two are left.
These are Chernuble and Count Margariz.

### 103

Strong, handsome, fast and agile, Margariz,
a very valiant knight, charged Oliver.
Under the golden boss he broke the shield
and ran his spearpoint close against his side,
but by God's grace he did not touch his flesh.
The spear-haft shattered, but he kept his seat,
and rode on past, unhindered. Then he blew
a clarion call to summon up his men.

*The conflict is now general:*

### 104

Fierce now the fighting, fierce and general.
Roland ignored all danger, struck out hard
with his strong spear until the spear-haft snapped
after fifteen encounters. Then he drew
sharp Durendal and spurred at Chernuble.
Down through the helmet where carbuncles shone,
down through cap, hair, eyes, face, through close-meshed mail
and through the man who wore it sank his blade,
down through the heathen's crutch, through saddle, rich
with beaten gold, straight through the horse's spine
  no pause to seek a joint - and there it stopped.
Down on the meadow grass he threw them dead,
both horse and man.
                    'Son of a serf!' he said.
'You fool, to come here! Will Mahomet help?
Such scum as this can never win the day!'

Now through the battlefield Count Roland rides.
He grasps good Durendal which carves and cuts
so sharp and deep, he slaughters Saracens.
Had you but seen him as he tossed them dead,
corpse upon corpse and the bright pools of blood
lie gleaming on the ground! Blood masked his mail,
it covered both his arms, covered the neck
and shoulders of his horse, brave Wideawake.
His comrade Oliver struck hard and swift,
the Twelve did not hang back, and all the Franks
struck home and struck again and infidels
fell dead or senseless on the battlefield.
'God prosper our good men!' the archbishop called,
and shouted out, 'Mountjoy!' the emperor's cry.

                                                                aoi

Through the fray too rode Oliver. His spear
had broken off, and with the stump he struck
a heathen called Malun, shattered his shield,
so gay with gold and flowers, made his two eyes
leap from their sockets and his brains splash down
onto his feet. With seven hundred more,
down to the ground he hurled the heathen dead.
Turgis he slaughtered next, then Esturguz.
The stump he held splintered and broke right off
close by the handgrip.
                    'What are you doing, friend?'
Count Roland cried. 'It's iron and steel we need,
not bits of wood, in such a fight as this.

Where's your sharp sword, gold hilt and crystal boss,
where's Halteclere?'
                              'Still in its sheath,' he said.
'Too much to do, I've not had time to draw!'

aoi


### 107

Oliver drew his sword as Roland urged
and showed him he could use it like a knight.
Down came its edge onto an infidel,
Justin of Stony Valley. In two halves
he split the heathen's head and split his trunk
and shining mail, split saddle rich with gold
and the good horse's spine.  Stone dead they fell
before him in the field.
                              'That's more like you,
my brother!' Roland cried. 'For blows like that
the emperor holds us dear.' And on all sides
the Frenchmen shout, 'Mountjoy!', great Charles' cry.

aoi

### 108

Gerin rode Sorrel, Gerier his friend
rode his good charger Deerswift. Both at once
they spurred, slacked rein, and at full gallop charged
the heathen Timozel. One hit the shield
and one the hauberk; both drove their sharp spears
into the heathen's flesh. Down he dropped dead,
and no one knows, I never could find out,
which was the faster, which one struck him first.
Dead fell Esperverès, son of Burel,
struck down by Engeler of Gascony;

and the archbishop killed their Siglorel.
He was the enchanter who'd already been
to visit hell before. By magic arts
Jupiter took him there. 'Forfeit to us,
that one!' the archbishop said. Roland replied,
'Son of a serf, he's finished! Oliver,
my friend and brother, how I love such blows!'

### 109

Sterner the battle still, and stronger blows
heathen and Franks exchange, these in attack,
the others in defence. How many spears
bloodied and broken, banners and pennons torn,
how many fine young Frenchmen lose their lives!
Never again will these men see their wives,
their mothers, or the Franks who wait for them
up in the mountain passes with the king.

aoi

### 110

Great Charles the emperor weeps. What use is that?
They'll get no help from him. Evil indeed
the service done his king by Ganelon
the day he sold his friends to King Marsile!
Both life and limb he lost for this at Aix,
where he was taken to be tried and hanged.
Hanged too with him were thirty of his kin,
men who had never thought to die like that.

aoi

### 111

Hard is the battle, hard and terrible.
Roland does marvels, so does Oliver,

Archbishop Turpin strikes a thousand blows.
None of the Twelve hang back, and all the Franks
unite in their attack. The heathen fall,
they fall and die in thousands. Flee or die,
that's all the choice they're given. And the French
lose their best champions, men who won't see
fathers or kin again, or Charlemagne,
the emperor waiting for them in the pass.
In France a storm arose, a storm so fierce
no one had seen its like. Winds roared and howled,
thunder crashed out, hailstones and drenching rain
fell in great torrents, and repeatedly
forked lightning blazed and struck. And, this is true:
an earthquake shook the ground. No building stood
from Michael-in-the-Peril right to Saintes
or from Besançon up to Wissant port*
whose walls did not collapse. Black darkness fell
and hid the sky at noon. There was no light
but when the heavens cracked. None could see this
and not be terrified.

         'The world is ending!'
many of them cried, 'this is the day of wrath!'
They were mistaken, but they could not know
that what they saw was grief for Roland's death.

### 112

Strongly and with good heart the French have fought.
The heathen dead lie heaped. Not two survive
of all their hundred thousand infidels.
'Our men are very valiant!' Turpin said.
'No one on earth has better. You can read

clearly enough in the *Exploits of the Franks**
that our great emperor's vassals are superb.'
They went about the field and sought their dead,
they wept for grief and sorrow, mourned their kin
in tenderness and love. As they did this,
up rode the king Marsile and all his men.

aoi

*Marsile appears in person to lead his second onslaught:*

### 113

Along a valley came the heathen king
with the great host he had mustered; huge, it was,
twenty divisions, counted. Sunlight flashed
and danced on all those helmets set with gems,
on gleaming shields, on hauberks bright inlaid,
and seven thousand bugles blew the advance.
Across the countryside their voices rang.
'Brother, we are betrayed,' Count Roland said.
'The traitor Ganelon has sworn our death,
no doubt about his guilt. The king will take
full and sufficient vengeance. We must fight
a harder battle than has yet been fought
under the arch of heaven. I shall use
my Durendal, and you, dear comrade, strike
with your bright Halteclere. How far across
the world we've borne them both, what battles won!
No one shall sing foul songs and laugh at them!'

aoi

*The archbishop brings down Abyss of Hell:*

### 114

Now King Marsile could see his men lie dead,
heaped in their slaughtered thousands. On he rode,
his horns and trumpets sounding, and drew near
with his whole mighty host. Before them all
rode out Abyss of Hell, a Saracen
more vile than any in that company.
Many his vices, terrible his crimes.
He has no faith in God, Saint Mary's son,
is black as molten pitch, loves treachery,
loves murder more than all Galicia's gold.
No one has ever seen him laugh or play.
Courage he has, and utter recklessness,
and these endear him to the heathen king.
He bore his dragon standard, onto which
his followers rallied. This was not a man
whom Turpin could approve. No sooner seen,
he longed to charge and strike.

                    'Heretical,'
he murmured to himself, 'that Saracen!
Best if I go and kill him. I don't like
cowards or cowardice, and never have.'

                                     aoi

### 115

The archbishop made first move. He rode the horse
he'd taken once in Denmark from a king,
Grosaille, whom he had killed there. Agile, swift,
this charger had flat legs and concave feet,
short thighs and good broad quarters; furthermore

it was deep-ribbed, straight-backed, had a white tail,
with yellow mane, small ears, and tawny head.
No living creature had the speed of it.
The archbishop spurred unflinching. None could check
his charge at Hell's Abyss. He rode and struck
strong as a miracle upon his shield.
This blazed with gems - topaz and amethyst,
carbuncles and *esterminals* which glowed
with their own light. The emir Galafès
had had it in Dread Valley from a fiend
and given it to Abyss. Turpin struck home,
holding back nothing, and that shield was then
not worth a penny, I can promise you.
He ran him through and through and dropped him dead
down on the empty ground.
                              'What valour there!'
exclaimed the Franks. 'The crozier's safe with him!'

*The French know they are overwhelmed:*

### 116

Whichever way they looked, the Franks could see
nothing but infidels. The countless hordes
swarmed over every space, and all the Franks
called out repeatedly to Oliver,
to Roland, to the Twelve, to bring them help.
But the archbishop spoke to them and said,
'My noble lords, take courage! In God's name
I beg you, do not run! Don't let good men
laugh at us in their songs. Today we die,
but let's die fighting, that's by far the best.
We know our death is sure. But this I say:

the gates of Paradise stand open wide
and wait to welcome you. There you shall sit
enthroned among the Holy Innocents!'
At this the Franks took heart, and there was none
who did not shout the battle-cry, 'Mountjoy!'

aoi

*Single combats, and the Peers fall:*

### 117

There was a Saracen among the host
from Saragossa - half that town was his -
and he was Climorin, no honest man.
(He took the traitor's oath and kissed his mouth,
gave helmet and carbuncle to him, vowed
he'd bring sweet France to shame and take the crown
from Charlemagne himself.) Amid the throng
he sits good Barbamusche, swifter than hawk,
faster than swallow's flight, and spurs him deep.
Rein loosened, at full gallop now he runs
at Engeler the Gascon of Bordeaux.
Mailshirt nor shield protect him. In his flesh
Climorin sets his spearpoint, thrusts and drives
the iron head right out behind his back.
Dead on the field he flung him, lance outstretched,
and cried aloud, 'These men are easy meat!
Strike at them, heathen, strike, break their array!'
'God, there's a good man gone!' the French exclaimed.

aoi

### 118

'Sir comrade,' Roland called to Oliver,
'Engeler's killed! One of our bravest men!'

'God send I can avenge him!' said the count,
and drove gold spurs into his horse's sides.
Down he brought Halteclere, blade red with blood,
thrust strongly sideways and threw Climorin
dead from his racing horse. Swift devils came
and took his soul away. Next the count killed
Duke Alphaien, and after that unhorsed
some seven Arabs who won't fight again,
and clean cut off Lord Escababi's head.
'My comrade is annoyed,' Count Roland said.
'He's doing as well as I can do myself.
It's for these blows the emperor values us!'
Aloud he cried, 'Strike at them, knights, strike hard!'

aoi

## 119

Up rode an infidel called Valdabrun,
godfather to the heathen king Marsile,
lord of four hundred dromonds on the sea.
Shipmen obey no other lord but him.
He took Jerusalem by treachery,
Solomon's holy Temple there profaned
and slew the patriarch beside the font.
This man received the oath from Ganelon,
gave him a thousand *manguns* and his sword.
He sits his warhorse Gramimund, who runs
faster than falcon's flight, drives in sharp spurs
and charges great Duke Samson. Through his shield,
through the linked hauberk deep into his flesh
he drove the spearhead, shaft and pennon too.
Dead from the saddlebow he tossed the duke,

and cried,

'On, heathen, on! They're easy prey!'
'Oh God, a bitter loss!' exclaimed the Franks.

aoi


### 120

Roland saw Samson fall. Great was his grief,
you can be sure of that. He spurred and charged;
gripping sharp Durendal, dearer than gold,
hard as he could he struck the infidel
high on his jewelled helm. Clean through his head,
through body, mailshirt, saddle bright with gold
he sank the steel. Deep in the horse's back
it came to rest. Both horse and man he killed,
grieve or rejoice who may.

'That's a harsh blow!'
the heathen cried.

'I can't approve your men,'
Count Roland said. 'You're arrogant and wrong.'

aoi


### 121

An African had come from Africa*,
his name Ill Thinking, son of King Ill Thought.
All his equipment blazed with beaten gold,
he glittered in the sunlight and outshone
all his companions. Now he sat his horse -
Lost Leap he called him, none could go so fast -
and charged Count Anséis. Full on his shield
through red and blue he struck, through links of mail;
into his body rammed both head and shaft.

Great Anséis is dead, his days are done.
'Alas for you, brave heart!' exclaim the French.

### 122

Across the field rode Turpin. Never clerk
existed who sang mass and who could strike
such blows as Turpin dealt!
                              'God's curse on you!'
cried the archbishop. 'Infidel, you've killed
a man whose loss goes to my very heart!'
He made his horse curvet, struck on the shield
of fine Toledan work and flung him dead
down on the meadow grass among the rest.

### 123

Next up came Grandonie, King Capuel's son,
of Cappadocia, riding Marmorie,
swifter than bird in flight. Slackening his rein,
the heathen spurred and charged and with great force
struck Gerin's scarlet shield. He shattered it,
broke it clean off his neck and drove his spear
and yellow pennon deep into his flesh,
tossing him dead onto a lofty rock.
Then he killed Gerier, Count Gerin's friend,
then Berenger; Guy of St Anthony;
and then he charged the great duke Austorie,
lord of Valence and honours on the Rhone.
Him too he killed. The infidels rejoiced.
'Many of ours are falling!' said the French.

Count Roland gripped his bloody sword. He heard
the Franks' distress and felt such bitter grief,
it all but broke his heart.

           'God damn you, slave!'
he cried. 'You'll pay for those!' Under the spur,
his eager horse leapt forward, and they met.

125

Valiant and strong was Grandonie, a knight
expert and brave. Confronting him he saw
Count Roland, whom he'd never seen before,
but knew at once by his fierce look, his face,
his build and noble bearing. Hard he tried
to keep his courage, but he failed; in vain
he sought to turn away. Roland hit hard,
split the whole helmet to the nosepiece, cut
through nose, mouth, teeth, through body clad in mail,
through gilded saddle and silver saddlebows
and sank the blade deep in the horse's back.
Dead past recovery he flung them both
and all the men of Spain cried out in grief.
'Our champion can hit hard!' exclaimed the Franks.

*The outnumbered French drive off the enemy:*

125a

Heavy and fierce the fighting. Frankish knights
strike with their burnished spears. Had you been there,
what grief and suffering you'd have seen, what pain!
So many men lay wounded, bleeding, dead,

face up, face down, one on another heaped.
No longer can the Saracens endure;
like it or not, forced from the field, they flee.
By their sheer strength, the Frenchmen drive them off.

aoi

*The conflict renewed; the French reduced to sixty men:*

126

Bitter and terrible the conflict. Franks
hit out in strength and anger, cut through wrists,
through ribs and spines, through steel to living flesh.
Red runs the blood across the tender grass.
'Great Land, Mahomet curse you! There's no race
more obstinate than yours!' the heathen cry.
Not one of them but shouts aloud,

'Marsile!

Ride, king, we need your help! Marsile, ride fast!'

127

'Comrade,' Count Roland said to Oliver,
'Turpin's a matchless knight, you must agree.
No one on earth can handle lance or spear
as Turpin does.'

'Let's help him, then!' he said,

and with these words the Franks renewed the attack.
Hard are the blows, bitter the clash of steel,
dreadful the Christian loss and suffering.
Oh, to have seen Roland and Oliver
slashing and cutting with their sharp-edged swords!
What wonders Turpin did with his strong spear!
The numbers are quite plain. It's written down

in documents and letters, say the *Deeds*:
they killed four thousand infidels and more.
In four assaults they triumphed. In the fifth
they suffered loss and sorrow. All the French
died then, except for sixty whom God saved.
Dearly those sixty men will sell their lives!

aoi

*Roland suggests they now call the emperor back; Oliver is bitterly*
*angry at the useless deaths, and refuses:*

### 128

Count Roland saw his many men lie dead
and said to Oliver, 'Comrade, dear friend,
for God's sake tell me, what can you suggest?
So many and so brave, all lying there!
Sweet France, now robbed of these and so bereft!
Oh Charles, beloved king, why weren't you here?
My brother Oliver, how can we send,
how can we tell the king?'
                          'I do not know.
But I will die before I'll be disgraced.'

aoi

### 129

'I'll sound the oliphant,' Count Roland said,
'and Charles will hear it up there in the pass.
He'll bring the Franks straight back, I promise you.'
'A shameful thing to do!' said Oliver.
'Your kin would be dishonoured. All their lives
they'd suffer that reproach. You wouldn't call
when first I asked you to; now I don't ask.
Call the king now, and that's sheer cowardice.

Look at your arms, both of them red with blood!'
'I've struck some good blows,' Roland answered him.

aoi

### 130

'We've a hard fight ahead,' Count Roland said.
'I'll blow the horn and Charlemagne will come.'
'A brave man would not do it!' said his friend.
'I asked you to; you wouldn't condescend.
If we had had Charles with us, then our men
would not be lying dead. No fault of theirs!
I tell you by my beard, if ever now
I see my sister Alda, you've no chance
of lying in her arms, be sure of that!'

aoi

### 131

'Why are you angry with me?' Roland asked.
'It's your own doing, comrade,' he replied.
'Courage used sensibly is not the same
as reckless bravery. Restraint does more
than mad heroics can. Franks lie there dead
because you were a fool. Never again
shall we serve Charles our king. If you'd agreed,
then Charles would have come back, have won the fight,
taken or killed Marsile. Fatal to us,
your mighty valour! Now no more we'll serve
great Charles - a man whose like will not be seen
from now till judgment day. Now you will die;
sweet France will be disgraced, and here today
our faithful friendship ends. Before tonight
in bitter anguish you and I must part.'

aoi

*The archbishop settles their quarrel and tells them to bring Charles back:*

### 132

The archbishop heard them arguing, drove in
his golden spurs, rode to rebuke them both:
'Lord Roland, and you too Lord Oliver,
I beg you in God's name, stop quarrelling!
No horn can help us now, but still it's best
to call the emperor back, he'll take revenge.
These men of Spain must not ride off in joy!
Our Frenchmen will dismount and find us dead,
our limbs lopped off; they'll load us onto biers
and on pack beasts, mourning they'll weep for us,
bury us safe in churchyards, so that dogs
and wolves and pigs don't make a meal of us.'
'That's good advice, my lord,' Count Roland said.

aoi

*Severely wounded as he is, Roland sounds the oliphant; it is this effort which will kill him:*

### 133

Count Roland set the mouthpiece to his lips,
tensed them, exerted all his strength, and blew.
High are the peaks and very long the note
which Roland blew. Full thirty leagues away
they heard the sound re-echo. Charlemagne
heard it as well and so did all his men.
'Ours are engaged!' he said.

                        'Ridiculous!'
said Ganelon at once. 'Indeed, a lie,
if any but yourself had spoken it.'

aoi

*Roland blows again, and the French hear it and turn to ride back:*

### 134

In pain and with great effort, Roland blew.
Blood spurted from his mouth, his temple cracked.
The great horn's note is strong and carries far;
in the high pass, Charles hears it. Naimon too
and all the other Franks can hear the call.
'That's Roland's horn!'said Charles.'He's been attacked.
He'd never blow for anything but that.'
'Attacked, what rubbish!' said Count Ganelon.
'Old and white-haired we know you are, but now
you sound quite childish. Surely you're aware
of Roland's arrogance! I cannot think
how God puts up with it. Don't you recall
how Roland took Neapolis, though you
had given no such orders? Out they came,
the Saracen defenders, and attacked
Roland the valiant. Afterwards he washed
the battlefield with water, turned the stream
to flow across it, hoping he could hide
his disobedience. Why, that horn of his,
he'll blow it all day long for just one hare!
He's showing off, I'm sure, before his peers.
What men on earth would dare to challenge him?
Come now, my lord, ride on! Why have you stopped?
The Great Land's still a very long way off.'                    aoi

### 135

His mouth is bloody and his temple gapes.
In pain and anguish Roland blows the horn.
King Charles can hear it, so can all the Franks.

'A long note, that,' said Charles.

        'A valiant man,'
Duke Naimon said, 'is using all his strength.
They are engaged, no question. And betrayed
by this man here, who wants you to ride on!
Arm, shout your battlecry, succour your men!
It's plain enough to hear: Roland's at bay.'

## 136

The emperor's bugles sound. The French dismount,
put on their hauberks, helmets, gold-rich swords.
Good shields they carry and strong heavy spears,
the pennons fluttering yellow, white and red.
The barons mount their chargers. All the host
ride spurring hard the whole length of the pass.
Not one but tells another,

        'If we reach
Roland before he dies, then how we'll fight
there at his side!' But what's the good of that?
They'll come too late, they have delayed too long.

## 137

The day drew on and brightened. Western sun
danced on the helms and hauberks, on fine shields
gay with well-painted flowers, dazzled on spears
and pennons richly gilt. In wrath rode Charles,
in wrath and grief the Franks. Not one but weeps,
not one but goes in dread for Roland's sake.
Count Ganelon's arrested. Charlemagne
called his head cook, Besgun, said,

'Guard him well!
He has betrayed my household.' Besgun set
a hundred of his kitchen hands, good men
and bad, to guard the count. They pulled out hair
from his moustache and beard; each punched him hard
four times; with sticks and staves they thrashed him well;
then put a collar round his traitor's neck
and chained him like a bear. On a pack beast,
dishonourably, they loaded Ganelon.
And so they'll keep him till Charles wants him back.

*The host rides full tilt through the mountains:*

### 138

High are the peaks, and full of shadows, dark          aoi
the deep ravines, the running waters swift.
In front and rear all the shrill bugles speak;
their myriad voices answer the oliphant.
Wrathful rides Charles, wrathful and sad the Franks.
Not one but weeps and mourns and prays to God
to guard Count Roland till they reach the field.
How they will fight beside him! What's the good?
They took too long, they cannot be in time.

                                                      aoi

### 139

In fury rides the king. Above his mail
he's spread his beard, white, clearly visible.
Deep spur the lords of France, each one enraged
that he's not there with Roland as he fights
the Saracens of Spain.

*Roland is dying. He prays for his fellows, and rides once more into battle:*

Roland is hurt,

his soul can't linger long. Those sixty men
he still has with him, God, how valorous!
Better no king or captain ever led.

aoi

### 140

Up hill and down Count Roland looked, and saw
the men of France lie dead. As a knight should,
he mourned them:

'Noble lords, may God above

have mercy on you, grant you Paradise,
give your souls rest among his holy flowers!
No better fighters have I ever seen
than you, my valiant lords. How many years
you've served me, what wide lands won for the king!
How tenderly, alas, he cherished you!
Dear land of France, so sweet, so much beloved,
and now bereft, dispeopled! You, her sons,
on my account you lie there dying, dead,
and I can't help or save you. God himself,
never untrue, come now and bring you help!
You, brother Oliver, I must not fail.
I shall die soon of grief, if I'm not killed.
Come with me, comrade, let's attack again.'

### 141

Into the battle Roland rode once more,
struck out with Durendal, cut clean in two
Faldrun of Puy and some two dozen more

of their best knights. No one before or since
has thirsted so for vengeance. Heathen fled
as deer before the hounds from his attack.
'Well done indeed!' cried Turpin. 'Every knight
who carries arms and rides on a good horse
should show this courage, should be fierce and strong
in conflict with the enemy, or else
the man is not worth fourpence, and must go
into a monastery and be a monk
and offer daily prayers for our sins.'
'Strike hard, spare none of them!' Roland replied,
and at his words the Frenchmen re-engaged.
Very great loss the Christians suffered now.

*King Marsile leads a fresh attack, but encounters Roland; loses his
sword-hand and his son, and flees:*

### 142

In such a battle, men who realise
that there's no hope of quarter, fight like lions,
and so the French did now, savage and fierce.
Among them suddenly, valiant, astride
his charger Watchdog, King Marsile appeared.
He spurred him well, charged Bevon lord of Beaune
and Dijon town, shattered his shield to bits,
broke through his mail and killed him at a blow.
Ivon and Ivorie he killed; with them
Gerard of Roussillon. Not far away
Roland was riding.
                            'Damn your soul to hell!'
he cried to King Marsile. 'You do great wrong
to kill my comrades, and you'll pay for it

before we part! Today you shall find out
what name they give my sword!' Strongly he struck
and slashed the king's right hand clean off his wrist.
Next the fair head of Jurfaret, his son,
he took with Durendal. The infidels
cried out,

   'Mahomet, save us! All our gods,
take vengeance on King Charles! He brought them here,
these stubborn men who'd rather die than run!'
Then, to each other, 'Come, let's get away!'
A hundred thousand of them turn and flee,
men who will not come back, call them who will.

                  aoi

*Marsile's uncle the caliph attacks the French:*

### 143

But what's the good of that? Marsile has gone,
but Marganice remains, the al-caliph.
He's lord of Carthage, Alfrere, Garmalie
and Ethiopia, a land accursed.
Black are his warriors, their noses broad,
ears large; they number fifty thousand men
and ride full tilt and furious. Now they shout
the heathen battle cry. Count Roland said,
'This is our martyrdom. Now I'm quite sure
we haven't long to live. Traitor is he
who doesn't sell his life dear as he can!
Strike with your shining swords, my lords, strike well!
Fight for your lives and deaths! Don't let sweet France
suffer disgrace for us! When Charles my lord
reaches the battlefield, then let him see

what punishment we gave the Saracens!
For each of us, he'll find fifteen of them
scattered around us dead, and bless our names.'

aoi

### 144

When Roland saw the accursed race approach,
blacker than ink, nothing about them white
except their teeth, he said,
                'Today we die,
no doubt of that. Follow me, Franks, attack!'
'Hell take the slowest!' said Count Oliver,
and at these words the French knights charged again.

*Oliver is mortally wounded:*

### 145

The heathen saw how few the Frenchmen were,
took courage and rejoiced. 'The emperor's wrong!'
they said among themselves. Now Marganice,
riding a sorrel, drove in golden spurs,
and from the rear charged Oliver. He pierced
the close-meshed mail and thrust the iron head
right through his chest.
              'There, that's a blow for you!'
the caliph cried. 'Unlucky was the day
your Charlemagne placed you here! He's done us wrong
and it's not right he should rejoice at it.
On you alone I've taken full revenge!'

### 146

He has his deathblow, Oliver knows that.
He grips bright Halteclere and brings its edge

down on the caliph's golden-pointed helm,
scatters the jewelled florets to the ground
and splits his head down to the small front teeth.
With a strong sideways thrust, he flung him dead,
cried out,
          'Heathen, to hell! I don't deny
King Charles has suffered loss, but you shan't go
and boast about it to your womenfolk
or say you took a pennyworth of loot
or injured me or any of my friends.'
Then he called out to Roland, wanting help.

                                      aoi

### 147

Count Oliver can feel that death is near.
He craves and thirsts for vengeance and attacks
deep in the thickest of the heathen throng.
What ashen spearhafts snap, what strong shields break,
what hands and feet fly off beneath his blade,
what saddles and what ribs he slashes through!
Any who saw him lop off heathen limbs
and toss dead infidels aside in heaps,
one corpse upon another, could be sure
he'd seen true valour there. Nor did the count
forget great Charles' battlecry, but loud
cried out, 'Mountjoy!' And then to Roland called,
to his dear friend and equal,
                      'Comrade, here!
In bitter pain today we two must part.'

                                      aoi

Count Roland looked into his comrade's face
and saw it livid, pale, discoloured, blue.
Bright blood streamed down his body, spurted, fell
in splashes on the ground.
                              'God,' said the count,
'I don't know what to do. Comrade, alas
for your great valour! No one equals you,
nor ever will do. Ah, sweet France, so stripped
of fighting men, bereft and destitute!
How this will harm the king!' As Roland spoke,
still in his saddle, he lost consciousness.

                                                    aoi

Roland sits senseless on his horse. Nearby
Count Oliver is dying. He has bled
so freely that his eyes are troubled; now
he cannot see to tell two men apart.
Roland came near; Oliver struck at him,
struck on the helmet rich with gems and gold,
from top to nosepiece cracked the helm in two,
but did not touch his head. Roland looked up,
kindly and gently asked him,
                              'Comrade, friend,
did you intend that blow? It's Roland here,
Roland who's always loved you. I don't think
you gave me any challenge.'
                              'That's your voice.
But I can't see you,' Oliver replied.
'The Lord God see you! Was it you I hit?

Brother, forgive the blow!'
                              'You did no harm,
none,' said his comrade. 'I forgive it you
here and before the face of God.' At this
the two men bowed. In such dear love they part.

### 150

Death's anguish gripped Count Oliver. His eyes
rolled in his head, hearing and sight were gone.
Now he dismounted, knelt down on the ground,
aloud and painfully confessed his sins,
pronounced his *mea culpa*. Palm to palm
he held his hands upraised and prayed to God
to grant him Paradise, to bless the king,
sweet France and Roland, comrade, more than all.
His heart stopped beating and his helmet fell
forward over his face. He lay full length
stretched on the ground. The count is dead and gone,
he'll make no more delay. Brave Roland wept
and grieved for Oliver. No sadder man
would you hear mourning anywhere on earth.

### 151

Count Roland saw that Oliver was dead,
looked at his body, face down on the ground,
softly began to mourn: 'Sir comrade, friend,
alas for all your valour! Such long years
our fellowship has lasted! In that time
you never did me wrong, nor did I you.
Now that you're dead, I grieve to be alive.'
Again he lost his senses, mounted still

astride good Wideawake. Go where he may,
the golden stirrups will not let him fall.

*All the French have fallen to the enemy except for Roland, Turpin
and Walter of Hum:*

### 152

Before he had recovered from his swoon,
while he was still unconscious, Roland lost
all the remaining Franks, except for two:
Turpin of Rheims and Walter, count of Hum,
who came down from the mountains, where he'd fought
long with the Saracens. His men were dead,
all conquered by the heathen. He'd no choice,
but fled down from the peaks and called for help,
called upon Roland:
                              'Ah, my noble lord,
brave count, where are you? Let me be with you,
and then I'm not afraid! It's Walter here,
old Droon's nephew, Maelgut's conqueror!
You used to love me for my valour. Now
my spearhaft's broken and my shield pierced through,
my hauberk ripped and torn, they've struck their spears
right through my body. Soon I shall be dead,
my life is done. Oh, but I sold it dear!'
As he said this, Count Roland heard his voice,
spurred and rode fast across the battlefield.                    aoi

*The three heroes attack the Moslem hordes:*

### 153

Grieving and full of anger, Roland drove
into the thickest of the heathen throng

and slaughtered twenty of the infidels.
Walter killed six, Archbishop Turpin five.
'How dangerous these are!' the heathen cried.
'My lords, make sure that none of them survive!
He's a foul traitor who does not attack,
a coward any man who lets them live!'
At this they raised once more their hue and cry,
and from all sides returned to the attack.

aoi

### 154

Count Roland was a noble warrior,
Walter of Hum a very valiant knight,
the archbishop brave and expert. None of them
would leave the others. Side by side the three
struck deep among the close-ranked infidels.
Round them were forty thousand mounted men;
a thousand men on foot; there was not one,
in my opinion, dared go near the three.
Lances they flung, and spears, shot arrows, darts,
all kinds of quarrels, javelins and bolts.
Count Walter died at once. They pierced the shield
on Turpin's shoulder, cracked his helm apart,
wounded him in the head, broke through his mail
and thrust four spearheads deep into his flesh.
His horse they killed beneath him. Ah, what grief,
what sorrow when Archbishop Turpin falls!

aoi

### 155

The moment Turpin fell, pierced by four spears,
he leaped up, looked for Roland, ran to him

and said,

        'I'm not defeated! No true knight
surrenders while he lives!' He drew his sword,
Almace, bright steel, and struck a thousand blows
and then still more wherever he could find
infidels closely clustered. Afterwards
Charles said that he'd spared none of them: they found
four hundred dead around him, slashed, run through
or with their heads cut off. The *Frankish Deeds*
record this. So does he who saw the fight,
being present on the field, the valiant Giles,
for whom God does such wonders*. It was he
who wrote the account in Laon monastery.
Any who don't know this are misinformed.

*Roland blows a last call on the oliphant; Charlemagne's bugles reply:*

### 156

Nobly Count Roland battles, but he's soaked
in sweat from head to foot, is burning hot,
and suffers agony from the cracked skull
he split apart, blowing the oliphant.
But still he wants to know if Charles will come,
so takes the horn and blows a wavering call.
Great Charles drew rein and listened.

                    'Hark, my lords,
the day goes very ill,' the emperor said.
'Roland is lost to us. That call's so faint,
I know he can't survive. Ride, every man
who wants to reach him, ride! All bugles sound!'
And sixty thousand high-pitched clarions call,
the mountains answer and the valleys ring.

The heathen hear their voices and they know
how great their danger. 'Charles is here!' they cry.

### 157

'The emperor's coming back!' the heathen say.    aoi
'Hark to their bugles! If King Charles attacks,
we'll lose too many men. If Roland lives,
there'll be no peace, he'll start the war again
and our fair Spain is lost!' Four hundred men
and all the pick of those there in the field
assembled and with all their strength attacked
Roland. And now he has enough to do!

aoi

*Roland and Turpin make a last stand:*

### 158

Seeing them come, he summons up his strength,
his power and courage. He won't turn away,
not while he lives. Deep into Wideawake
he drives his golden spurs and charges home
into the heathen mass. Turpin and he
call to each other, 'Come on, friend, this way!
Hark to the Frankish horns! Great Charlemagne
is coming back to us, the mighty king!'

### 159

Cowards or proud men Roland never liked,
nor worthless evil men, nor any knight
lacking in knightly valour. So he said
to Turpin there beside him,

'You, my lord,

have lost your horse, I'm mounted. For your love
I'll make my stand with you. Both good and bad
we'll take together. I won't stir a step,
no one can make me leave you. All their blows
we'll pay them back, and more. Sharp Durendal
is stronger than them all!' Turpin replied,
'Call him a traitor who hangs back! The king
is on his way and he'll take full revenge!'

### 160

'Alas that we were born!' the heathen cried.
'A dark day this for us! We've lost our lords,
lost friends, and now Charlemagne is coming here
with all his host. How clear their bugles sound,
how loud they shout, 'Mountjoy'! Count Roland's more
than any man can conquer! Once again
let's shoot at him, and after that let's go!'
In they rained lances, quarrels, arrows, darts
and heavy spears. They pierced Count Roland's shield,
broke through the chainmail, did not touch his flesh,
but Wideawake fell dead with thirty wounds
under his rider. Then the heathen fled,
leaving Count Roland where he stood, unhorsed.

aoi

*Hearing the returning host, the Moslems flee;*
*Roland gathers up the bodies of his comrades:*

### 161

In rage and fury now the heathen fled
and made all haste to get away to Spain.
Count Roland had no means of hunting them,

his horse was dead, he had to go on foot.
Instead he went to help Turpin of Rheims,
unlaced his gold-rich helm and took it off,
took off his light-weight mailshirt, cut away
his silken tunic. Then he used the silk
to pack his gaping wounds. Close in his arms
he held him to his chest and lowered him
softly and tenderly onto the grass.
Most gently then Count Roland said to him,
'Noble archbishop, will you give me leave?
Our comrades are all dead, the men we loved.
We mustn't leave them lying where they fell.
I want to go and find them, bring them here,
and lay them decently in front of you.'
'Go,' said the archbishop, 'and come back again.
This field is yours, thanks be to God, and mine.'

### 162

Count Roland turned away and all alone
searched through the battlefield, up hill, down dale,
found Gerin, Gerier and Berenger,
found Otho, then Duke Samson, Anséis,
and Gerard the Old Man of Roussillon.
All these he lifted, brought them one by one
and laid them in a row at Turpin's feet.
Turpin could not but weep. He raised his hand,
blessed them and said,
                    'Alas for you, my lords!
The God of glory give your spirits rest
among the holy flowers of Paradise!

Death's anguish grips me hard. I shall not see
noble King Charles, the mighty emperor.'

### 163

Back to the field went Roland, searched again,
until he found his comrade Oliver.
Against his chest he held him in his arms,
as best he could carried the body back
and laid it by the others on a shield.
Turpin absolved and signed them with the cross.
Sharper the sorrow still, harsher the grief!
Count Roland spoke:
           'Fair comrade Oliver,
son of Duke Renier who held the fief
of Val de Runiers on the border march,
no better knight exists in any land.
Whether at breaking lances, piercing shields,
or vanquishing and bringing down the proud,
or giving aid and counsel to good men
and utterly defeating heathen scum,
you, brother Oliver, outdid them all.'

### 164

When Roland saw his fellows lying dead
and Oliver his comrade whom he loved,
compassion filled him, he began to weep.
He lost all colour, could not stand for grief,
despite himself fell fainting to the ground.
'Alas for you, brave heart!' the archbishop cried.

*Death of Turpin:*

### 165

Archbishop Turpin, seeing Roland faint,
suffered a sharper grief than any yet.
He put his hand out, took the oliphant;
he'd go, he thought, for water to a stream
that runs in Roncevaux, and bring it back,
give some of it to Roland. Shakily,
one step and then another, Turpin tried
to reach the stream, but could not. He had lost
such quantities of blood, he was too weak.
In less time than it takes to walk along
a furrow's length, the archbishop's heart gave out,
and so he fell. Death's anguish gripped him fast.

### 166

Roland recovered, rose, though with great pain,
looked up the hillside, down, and on the grass
beyond his comrades, saw the baron lie,
God's own archbishop, chosen in His name.
Turpin confessed his sins and then looked up,
raised his joined hands to heaven, prayed to God
to grant him Paradise. Turpin is dead,
great Charles's warrior. Unceasingly
he fought the infidels in word and deed,
both by fine sermons and on bloody fields.
God in his gracious mercy give him rest!

aoi

Roland looked down at Turpin where he lay,
looked at the spilling guts and at the brains
that bubbled from his forehead, crossed his hands,
so white and beautiful, high on his chest
and mourned him bitterly, as Frenchmen mourn:
'Ah, valiant knight, son of a noble house,
now I commend you to the glorious king.
None readier to serve him will he find!
No such a prophet has there ever been
since the apostles lived, none with such power
to draw men to him and uphold the faith.
God grant your soul lack nothing, may the gates
of Paradise stand wide to welcome it!'

*Death of Roland:*

168

Roland could feel that death was very near.
Brain matter issued from his ears. He prayed
to God to call his comrades home, and next
prayed for himself to the angel Gabriel.
Then, to avoid all blame, he took the horn
and Durendal his sword, one in each hand,
and walked a crossbow-shot and more towards Spain.
He climbed a hill, came to a noble tree
which rose up tall above four marble slabs,
and here he fell face upward on the grass
and lost his senses, for his death was close.

High are the peaks and very high the trees
and under them four slabs of marble gleam.
On the green grass, unconscious, Roland lies.
And all the time an infidel had watched,
had smeared himself with blood, was shamming dead.
Now hurriedly he rose and ran across.
A strong man, very handsome, valorous,
through pride he came to lunacy and death.
He seized Count Roland, grasped bright Durendal,
cried out,
      'He's beaten, Charlemagne's nephew's dead!
I'll take this sword of his to Araby.'
His tugging roused Count Roland from his swoon.

Roland could feel him pulling at his sword,
opened his eyes, said,
      'You're not one of ours,
I'm sure of that,' and with the oliphant,
which he was firmly grasping, struck the man
hard on the helmet rich with gems and gold.
Steel, head and skull he shattered, forced both eyes
out of their sockets, dropped the heathen dead
there at his feet.
      'Infidel slave!' he said.
'How could you dare to touch me, right or wrong?
Any who hear of this will think you're mad.
I've cracked my oliphant across the bell
and all the gold and crystal's broken off.'

Now Roland realised his sight was gone.
He struggled to his feet, called up his strength;
his face had lost all colour. On a stone
that stood there dark before him, Roland struck
in bitter grief ten blows with Durendal.
Steel grated on the stone, but would not break
or notch.
       'Ah,' cried the count, 'St Mary, help!
Ah, Durendal, fine sword, alas for you!
I'm dying now, I can't take care of you.
How many battles have we won, what lands
conquered together for white-bearded Charles!
May no man own you who would ever run
in fear from any foe! Many long years
the best of fighters owned you. Never now
will holy France see such another man.'

Count Roland struck on the sardonyx stone;
the steel blade scraped and grated, would not break.
Then when he saw he could not damage it,
he spoke in lamentation, murmuring:
'Ah Durendal, how white and fair you are
how you give back the sunlight, how you blaze!
King Charles was in the vale of Maurienne
when by his angel God sent him command
to give you to a captain of his hosts.
Mighty and noble king, it was to me
he gave the sword, fastened it at my side.
For him I won with it Anjou and Maine,

free Normandy I won and Brittany,
I took Poitou, Provence and Aquitaine.
With Durendal I won him Lombardy,
Flanders, Bavaria and Burgundy,
the whole Romagna and Apulia.
Constantinople too I took for Charles,
they did him homage; and in Saxony
they all obey him and his word is law.
The Scots and Irish lands I took as well
and England too, his private property*.
What lands, what countries I have won with this,
lands which King Charles now holds!  Sorrow and grief
fill me for Durendal. I'd rather die
than let the heathen have it. God above,
keep France from such a loss, from such disgrace!

### 173

On a dark stone he struck, and cut away
more of the rock than I can tell you. Still
the grating blade refused to notch or break
and sprang back high undamaged off the stone.
When the count saw he could not break his sword,
softly he mourned it to himself and said,
'Ah, Durendal, how beautiful you are,
how holy too!  What relics you contain
inside your golden pommel - Peter's tooth,
some of St Basil's blood, St Denis' hair,
part of Our Lady's clothing. It's not right
for heathens to possess you. Christian hands
should use and care for you. May you not pass
into a coward's keeping when I'm gone!

Wide lands I've won with you, lands Charles holds now,
lands which have made him rich and powerful.'

### 174

Roland could feel death's hold grow tighter still;
it gripped his head, then shifted to his heart.
To a tall pine he ran, and under it
lay prone on the green grass, with sword and horn
held safely under him. He turned his head
so that he faced to Spain, and then the king
and all his men would say the noble count
had died a conqueror. Repeatedly
Roland confessed his sins and for their sake
held out his glove and offered it to God.

aoi

### 175

Roland could feel his time was almost gone.
High on a mountain peak he faced towards Spain,
with one hand struck his breast and said aloud,
'God, I confess my fault before your face
for all the sins I've done, both great and small,
since I was born, till now when I'm struck down.'
He held out his right glove for God to take.
Angels came down to him from heavens' height.

aoi

### 176

Under a pine lay Roland, facing Spain.
Much came into his mind - the many lands
he'd conquered valiantly, sweet France, the men
belonging to his lineage, Charles his lord

who'd brought him up. He could not help but weep
and cry for these. But for himself as well
he prayed, confessed his sins, begged mercy, said:
'Sole Image of the Father, full of truth,
St Lazarus you brought again from death,
saved Daniel from the lions - save my soul
from all the dangers my own sins have caused!'
His righthand glove he offered up to God.
Gabriel came and took it from his hand.
His head dropped on his arms. Hands joined, he died.
God sent his angel Cherubim, sent too
St Michael of the Peril, and with these
came holy Gabriel. They took his soul
and carried it with them to Paradise.

*Charlemagne and the French reach the battlefield:*

### 177

Roland is dead, in heaven God has his soul.
Charles reaches Roncevaux. No track or path,
no open ground, no yard or foot of land,
but bodies lie there dead, heathen and Franks.
'Nephew, where are you?' cried the emperor.
'Where's the archbishop? Where's Count Oliver?
Where are the friends Gerin and Gerier?
And where is Otho, where's Count Berenger?
Ivon and Ivorie whom I loved well?
The Gascon Engeler, where has he gone?
Where are Duke Samson and brave Anséis?
Gerard, Old Man of Roussillon, where's he?
All the Twelve Peers I placed here, where are they?'
But what's the use, when nobody replies?

'Ah God,' cried Charles, 'if only I'd been here
when the attack began!' He tugged his beard
in rage and fury, and his barons wept.
Down to the ground some twenty thousand fell
senseless. In great distress, Duke Naimon watched.

### 178

There's not a knight or baron in the host
who does not weep and bitterly lament.
They mourned their sons, their brothers, nephews, friends,
and their liege lords, all dead. Many collapsed
unconscious on the ground. But Naimon spoke,
wise man, and said to Charles,
                              'Look over there!
Two leagues away from us, those dusty roads,
that's where the heathen are. Now ride, my lord!
Ride and avenge our grief!'
                              'Ah God,' said Charles,
'they've a good start, those men! Now do me right!
The flower of France I've lost to them.' At once
he gave command to Otun, Gebuin,
to Theobald of Rheims and Milo:
                              'Guard
the hills and valleys, keep the battlefield.
Leave the dead lying as they are. Make sure
no lions or other animals get in,
none of the boys or squires. Let none set foot
upon the battlefield, not till God wills
that we return here.' Kindly and with love
they said,
          'Just king, dear lord, be sure we will.'
With them they kept one thousand of their knights.          aoi

*Charlemagne hunts down the Moslems:*

### 179

The emperor's bugles sound and on he rides,
leading his mighty host. The men of Spain,
backs turned, fled from them and as one the Franks
spurred on in hot pursuit. Then the king saw
the evening drawing on; he left his horse,
knelt down on the green grass and prayed to God
to stop the sun for his sake, hold night back
and keep the daylight. Lo, an angel came,
who often talked with him, and promptly said,
'Up, Charles, and ride! You shall have light. God knows
you've lost the flower of France. Take your revenge
upon this guilty race!' At his command
the emperor remounted and rode on.

aoi

### 180

A great and mighty work God did for Charles,
for now the sun stood still. The heathen fled;
hotly the Franks pursued, and in Dark Vale
began to catch them up. Towards the town
they drove them, killing as they went; they filled
their roads and highways, forcing them to ride
out of their way onto the river bank.
Deep, swift and dangerous the Ebro ran.
There were no boats, no barges, dromonds, none.
On Tervagant they called, a god of theirs,
and leaped into the flow. He gave no help!
The heaviest in full armour sank at once,

others were swept downstream. Most fortunate,
those who drank so much water that they drowned
in pain and anguish. None of them survived.
'Roland, alas for you!' the Frenchmen cried.

aoi

*Vengeance achieved, Charlemagne and his host encamp:*

### 181

When the king saw the heathen were all dead,
some by the sword, most drowned - excellent spoils
his knights won there - he then dismounted, knelt,
and thanked Almighty God. When he stood up
the sun had set.
                    'We must make camp,' said Charles.
'It's too late now to get to Roncevaux.
Our horses are exhausted, they must rest.
Unsaddle, free their heads, let them cool down
here in the meadows.' And the Franks replied,
'Yes, you are right, my lord,' and so obeyed.

aoi

### 182

Charles chose his resting place. The Franks dismount
in empty country, lift the saddles off,
take golden reins over the horses' heads
and turn them loose to graze on fresh green grass.
They've nothing else but that to offer them.
Exhausted men lie on the ground and sleep.
No watch of any kind they set that night.

Charles lay down in the meadow, his great spear
close by his head. He meant to sleep that night
without unarming, kept his hauberk on,
bright damascened and shining, laced his helm,
jewelled and rich with gold; and at his side
he fastened Joyous, his unequalled sword,
a sword which changes hue and flashes bright,
shedding new brilliance thirty times a day.
We know about the lance with which Our Lord
was wounded on the cross - Charles, God be thanked,
possessed its point, and he had had this set
inside the golden pommel. It was this
gave it its glory and its excellence
and the name Joyous. This the Frankish lords
must not forget. That's why they cry, 'Mountjoy!',
why none can stand before a French attack*.

Clear was the night and moonlit. Charles lay still,
but grieved for Roland, grieved for Oliver,
wept for the Twelve and all the Frankish lords.
Bloody and dead they lay at Roncevaux.
He could not help but suffer, and he prayed
to God to guard their souls. Charles was worn out,
he could endure no more. At last he slept.
In all the meadows now Franks lie asleep.
No horse can keep its feet; if they want grass,
they crop it as they lie. Much has he learned
who knows hard work and sorrow at first hand.

*Charlemagne dreams:*

185

Charles slept like one exhausted. Gabriel
was sent by God to guard him, and all night
stayed by his head. He showed him in a dream.
how an attack would soon be made on him;
and showed him too the dread significance.
Charles in his vision looked into the sky,
saw thunder, wind and hail, saw raging storms,
saw flames of fire and lightning all prepared.
These suddenly rained down upon his host.
Spearhafts of ash and apple flamed alight,
shields to their golden bosses burned away,
strong spearhafts snapped and shattered, helmets rang,
linked chainmail grated. Charles in deep distress
watched his knights struggle. After that there fell
leopards and bears upon them, open-mouthed,
vipers and other snakes and devils too,
dragons and griffins thirty thousand strong.
Not one but stooped out of the blazing sky
and seized a Frankish knight.
                          'Help us, great Charles!'
cried out his Franks, and he, unhappy king,
did all he could to reach them, but in vain.
Out from a forest came a lion, huge,
savage and fierce, a formidable beast.
This attacked Charles himself. The two gripped arms,
ready to try a fall, but which will stand,
which of them be thrown down, Charles cannot tell.
The emperor slept on and did not wake.

Another vision came. He was in France,
at Aix, and on a terrace in two chains
he saw a bear cub held. From the Ardennes
came thirty other bears, who spoke like men:
'My lord,' the creatures said, 'give him to us.
It's wrong for you to have him. He's our kin,
we owe him our support.' But as they spoke,
out from the royal palace raced a hound,
chose and attacked the largest of the bears
on the green grass beyond its fellows. Charles
watched the amazing conflict, could not tell
which of the beasts would win, the hound or bear.
It was God's angel showed this to the king.
Great Charles slept on till morning and bright day.

*The scene shifts to Saragossa:*

187

The heathen king Marsile fled all the way
to Saragossa. By an olive tree
in the cool shade he left his horse, put off
his sword, his helm and hauberk. Wretchedly
he lay down on the grass. His hand is gone,
his right hand, clean cut off; the stump still bleeds.
In anguish and from loss of blood he faints.
Out came Queen Bramimonde to meet her lord -
she shrieked, she wept, how bitterly she grieved!
And with her grieved some twenty thousand knights,
cursed Charles, cursed France, ran to Apollin's crypt,
insulted and reproached him angrily:

'You wicked god, why have you shamed us so?
This is our king, why let the Frenchmen win?
Whoever serves you well gets little pay!'
They took away his sceptre and his crown,
they hung him on a column by his hands,
then flung him to the ground beneath their feet
and beat and battered him with heavy clubs.
From Tervagant they took his carbuncle
and threw Mahomet down into a ditch
where pigs and dogs trampled and gnawed at him.

### 188

Marsile regained his senses, had his men
carry him up the stairs to his own room,
a vaulted chamber, painted and inscribed
with many colours. Bramimonde the queen
wept for him, tore her hair, declared her grief.
'Alas, poor Saragossa!' loud she shrieked.
'Ah, wretched loss, the noble king, your lord!
Today our gods turned traitors, criminals,
they failed him on the battlefield. Alas,
now if the emir doesn't fight those men -
so fierce are they that neither life nor death
matter to them at all! - what cowardice,
what weakness he will show! The emperor
is old, white-bearded, brave! And reckless too -
if there's a battle, he won't turn from it.
There's no one who can kill him, more's the shame!'

*Long ago Marsile sent for the Emir Baligant:*

### 189

In his great might the emperor seven years
waged war in Spain, captured its towns and towers.
Marsile the king did everything he could:
in the first year had letters sealed and sent
to Baligant who ruled in Babylon*.
This was the emir of antiquity,
of such enormous age that he'd outlived
Homer and Virgil both. He must bring help,
must come to Saragossa, said the king.
If he did not, Marsile would leave his gods,
forsake his idols, take the Christian faith
and seek a pact with Charles the emperor.
But Baligant was far away, and slow.
From forty kingdoms he called up his men,
had his great dromonds readied, barges, skiffs,
his galleys and his ships. Under the town
of Alexandria right on the sea
a harbour stands, and in it Baligant
prepared his navy. Then at last in May
on the first day of summer, with his fleet
the emir Baligant put out to sea.

*Baligant's fleet approaches the coast of Spain:*

### 190

Huge are the forces of this evil race.
Swiftly they sail, they row, they steer their ships.
High on each masthead and each lofty prow
bright blazing lanterns and carbuncles* shine

and cast a glory over all the sea.
And as the fleet drew near the coast of Spain
the shoreline shone and sparkled in its light.
This news was brought at once to King Marsile.

aoi

### 191

Not for a moment did the heathen pause.
They sailed out of salt water into fresh,
left first Marbrise and then Marbrose behind,
and sailing on upstream they brought their fleet
right up the River Ebro. All night long
the lanterns and carbuncles lit their way.
They came to Saragossa with the dawn.

aoi

*Baligant disembarks:*

### 192

Clear and unclouded shone the morning sun.
The emir left his lighter, disembarked
and from the starboard side stepped into Spain*.
Kings, seventeen of them, came after him,
and then more dukes and counts than I can tell.
Under a laurel growing in a field
they threw a white silk carpet on the grass
and on it placed a stool of ivory.
The emir Baligant here took his seat
but all the others stood. Their lord spoke first:
'Now listen to me, free and valiant knights!
King Charles the Frankish emperor shall not eat
unless I tell him to. All over Spain

he's made great war on me. Now I intend
to hunt him down in France. I shall not cease
from now until I die till Charles is killed
or begs me for his life!' In emphasis
he smacked his right glove down onto his knee.

193

Having said this, he went on to declare
that nothing in the world, not all its gold,
should stop him going to Aix, where Charles held court
and gave his judgments. The emir's men approved
and recommended this. Next Baligant
called out two of his knights, one Clarifan,
and Clarien his brother.
                              'You are sons,'
the emir said, 'of Maltraien the king,
who was my willing messenger. Go now
to Saragossa. Tell Marsile I've come
to help him fight the Franks. Let me find Charles
and great shall be the battle! Take this glove,
gold-lined and rich, and give it to Marsile;
it must be worn on his right hand; make sure!
Give him this golden baton. He must come,
do homage for his fief; and then I'll go
and strike Charlemagne in France. The king shall kneel,
beg mercy at my feet, abandon Christ,
or I shall have the crown off his white head.'
'Well said indeed, my lord,' the heathen say.

### 194

Now ride, my lords,' commanded Baligant.
'One of you take the baton, one the glove.'
'Dear lord, we will,' they answered, and they rode
till they reached Saragossa. Through ten gates,
over four bridges and through all the streets
where the townspeople lived, the two men rode.
As they went up towards the citadel
they heard an outcry by the palace - crowds
of heathen shrieked and wailed, mourning their gods,
Mahomet, Tervagant and Apollin,
whom they no longer had.
                              'Alas,' they cried,
'what will become of us? We are destroyed!
Marsile is lost to us, we have no king,
yesterday Roland cut his sword-hand off.
And fair-haired Jurfaret, we've lost him too.
The whole of Spain lies at the Frenchmen's feet!'
Baligant's men dismounted by the steps.

### 195

Under an olive tree they left their mounts;
two heathen took the reins. Then up they climbed,
holding each other by the cloak, and reached
Marsile's high palace. Then in honest love,
entering his vaulted chamber, these two men
gave him an evil greeting:
                              'Tervagant,
Mahomet our protector, Apollin,

save and defend the king and keep the queen!'
'What rubbish do I hear?' said Bramimonde.
'Those gods of ours are beaten. Evil work
they did at Roncevaux - they let our knights
be slaughtered by the Franks, they failed my lord
in the great battle there. He's lost his hand,
his right hand, look, it's gone, Roland did that.
Charles will command all Spain, and as for me,
unhappy prisoner, what am I to be?
And I've no man to take my wretched life!'

aoi

### 196

'Madam, don't say such things!' said Clarien.
'We two are messengers from Baligant.
He will stand by Marsile; he tells you this.
In token here he sends his glove and staff.
Four thousand lighters float on Ebro's flood,
barges and skiffs, fast galleys, dromonds, more
than I can tell you. Great and powerful
is the emir Baligant! He means to go
and find King Charles in France, and Charles shall die
or beg for mercy at the emir's feet!'
'No need to go so far!' said Bramimonde.
'You can find Franks much nearer you than that.
Seven long years they've been here, making war.
A valiant man, their emperor, and brave!
He'd rather die than quit the battlefield.
There's not a king on earth but seems to him
less than a child. He fears no living soul.'

'Enough of that!' said King Marsile. 'My lords,
address yourselves to me. As you can see,
my wound is fatal, I shall soon be dead.
I have no son, no daughter, nobody
who can inherit. Yesterday I had,
but he was killed. Fetch my lord here to me.
He has rights over Spain, and I renounce
my kingdom in his favour. Let him take
and then defend the realm against the Franks.
He can defeat Charlemagne inside a month;
I'll tell him how. Take Saragossa's keys;
say, if he trusts me, he won't go away.'
'My lord,' the envoys said, 'you speak the truth.'

aoi

### 198

'Charlemagne has killed my men,' said King Marsile,
'harried my lands, ravaged and sacked my towns.
Tonight he sleeps by Ebro, seven leagues -
no more than that, I counted them - from here.
Through you I tell the emir: Bring your host,
attack him there.' He handed them the keys.
The messengers bowed low, took leave and left.

*The messengers report to Baligant:*

### 199

They mounted and rode fast out of the town.
In anxious haste they came to Baligant
and offered him the keys.

                    'Make your report,'

he said. 'Where's King Marsile? I sent for him.'
'Wounded to death,' said Clarien. 'King Charles
yesterday crossed the passes, going home
towards sweet France, and in his rear he placed
a noble guard: Count Roland, Oliver,
all the Twelve Peers and twenty thousand Franks.
Valiant Marsile gave battle. On the field
he and Count Roland met. With Durendal
Roland struck off his swordhand. And he killed
his much loved son, and killed as well the lords
Marsile had led to battle. Marsile fled
and left the field, for he could do no more.
Charlemagne pursued him hotly. Now the king
tells you to come and help him; he resigns
the realm of Spain to you.' Great Baligant
considered and reflected. Such his grief,
in his distress he all but lost his mind.

aoi

## 200

'Lord emir,' said the envoy, ' yesterday
they fought at Roncevaux. Count Roland's dead,
and so is Oliver, so are the Twelve,
whom Charles so highly prized. And of their Franks,
some twenty thousand fell. But King Marsile
had his right hand cut off and was pursued
closely by Charlemagne. In all this fief
no knights are left alive. They were all killed
or else they drowned in Ebro. On its bank
the Franks have made their camp. They've put themselves
so near us in this country, if you wish

you can make certain none of them go home.'
Fierce then the emir's look, joyful his heart!
He got up from the faldstool, cried aloud:
'Barons, out of the ships! Now mount and ride!
Today, if that old emperor doesn't run
and hide himself, Marsile shall have revenge. ·
For his right hand, I'll give him Charles' head!'

*Baligant rides to Saragossa and accepts the kingdom of Spain from
Marsile:*

### 201

The heathen Arabs poured out of their ships,
mounted their mules and horses and rode out;
what else was there to do? Then Baligant,
having set them in motion, called an aide,
a trusted man, Gemalfin, said to him:
'Marshal my troops, I put you in full charge.'
Mounting one of his coursers, then he rode,
four dukes as escort, till he reached the town.
Here by a marble terrace he dismounts,
while four counts hold his stirrup, and goes up
the staircase to the palace. Bramimonde
came running out to meet him, said,
                                        'Alas!
In what disgrace and shame I've lost my lord!'
Down at his feet she fell; he lifted her.
They climbed in sorrow up to Marsile's room.

aoi

### 202

When King Marsile saw Baligant, he called
two of his Spanish Saracens and said,

'Lift me. Take both my arms and sit me up.'
In his left hand he took a glove and said,
'My lord emir and king, into your hands
I give the whole of Spain. City and fief,
I give you Saragossa. I've destroyed
my people and myself.'

       'Deeply I grieve,'
answered great Baligant. 'I cannot stay,
we have no time to talk, Charles will not wait.
But I accept your glove.' Such was his grief
that as he turned and went away, he wept.

                  aoi

### 203

Down the stone steps he ran, mounted, spurred hard,
caught up his men and passed them. As he rode,
he turned his head time and again and cried,
'My heathen, ride! The Franks are on the run!'

                  aoi

*Charlemagne and the French return to Roncevaux, mourn and bury
the dead:*

### 204

As early dawn was breaking, Charles awoke.
St Gabriel, who guarded him for God,
lifted his hand and signed him with the cross.
The king undid his armour, put it off,
and all his men throughout the host unarmed.
They mounted and rode hard by endless paths,
by broad tracks and wide roadways, till they came

at last to Roncevaux, and there they saw
the place of slaughter where the battle was.

aoi

### 205

King Charles rode into Roncevaux.  He wept.
to see the many dead, and told his Franks:
'Rein in, my lords, and walk. I must ride on
and find my nephew. I remember once
at the high feast at Aix, my valiant knights
were boasting of great battles bravely fought -
there I heard Roland telling them that he
would never die in any foreign land
if he did not go further than his peers,
his men and vassals. Face towards the foe,
far out ahead of them he'd lie in death,
a conqueror.' A stone's throw out in front
King Charles rode on, and up a steep incline.

### 206

As he rode searching for his nephew, Charles
noticed the meadow plants all flowering red
with blood shed by our Franks.* For pity's sake,
the king could not but weep. Then, riding on,
he saw and recognised beneath two trees
strong Roland's blows, struck in three blocks of stone.
On the green grass he saw his nephew lie.
Small wonder if he suffered! Down he got,
ran to his nephew, grasped him with both hands,
fainted in agony across the corpse.

King Charles came to himself. Naimon the duke,
Count Acelin with Geoffrey of Anjou
and Thierry, Geoffrey's brother, took the king
and helped him to his feet beneath a pine.
He looked down at his nephew lying dead.
Softly he spoke his sorrow:

                    'Roland, friend,
God give you mercy! None has ever seen
a knight more able to engage and win
the greatest battles. All my honour now
turns to decay.' So bitter was his grief,
do what he would, he fainted once again.

                                             aoi

### 208

The king regained his senses. Lifting him,
his four lords held him up. Down on the ground
he saw his nephew lie, so strong, well built,
his face quite colourless and eyes rolled back,
sightless and dark. In love and faith he mourned:
'Beloved Roland, God now set your soul
among the flowers of Paradise, in joy
and glory with the saints! An evil hour,
my lord, brought you to Spain!* No single day
will pass but I shall mourn you. All my strength
and joy must vanish now. I've nobody,
none to support my honour - not a friend
anywhere here on earth! Kinsmen perhaps,
but of such valour, none.' Handfuls of hair
the mourning king pulled out, and with him wept,
compassionate, a hundred thousand Franks.

                                           aoi

'Beloved Roland, I'll go home to France,
and when I'm in my room at Laon there
vassals from foreign realms will come and ask,
'Where is your captain general, where's the count?'
And I shall say, 'He's dead, he died in Spain.'
In great grief now I'll hold my many lands.
Daily for ever shall I mourn and weep.'

'Roland, so dear, so valiant, young and fair!
I shall be in my chapel there at Aix,
vassals will come and ask for news of you -
and I shall tell them, dreadful, terrible:
Dead is the man who won so much for me,
my sister's son! The Saxons will rebel,
so will the Bulgars and Hungarians,
and other evil races, and the men
of Africa, Palermo, Califerne,
and the Romagna and Apulia.
What troubles now begin, how great my need!
Who is there strong enough to rule my hosts
when he that always captained us is dead?
Sweet France, alas, how you are orphaned now!
My grief's too great to bear, would I could die!'
Charles plucked his hair in handfuls from his head,
tore his white beard. A hundred thousand Franks
in grief for him fell senseless to the ground.

'Dear Roland, God have mercy on your soul
and set it with the saints in Paradise!

The man who killed you leaves France desolate.
On my account my household dies - my grief
is such I do not want to live. Ah God,
St Mary's son, listen and grant this prayer -
before I reach the mountain pass at Cize,
let my soul leave my body, let it rest
in Paradise with theirs and let my flesh
be buried here beside them in one grave!'
The tears poured down his face, he pulled his beard.
Duke Naimon said,

               'Charles is in great distress.'

                                      aoi

## 212

'Lord emperor,' said Geoffrey of Anjou,
'you must control your grief. Have the field searched,
have all our comrades whom the heathen killed
buried together in a common grave.'
'Yes, blow your horn,' said Charles. 'Let it be so.'

                                        aoi

## 213

Count Geoffrey blew, and at the king's command
the French dismounted. Then at once they searched,
and carried all the bodies of their friends
to one large grave. Bishops and priests were there,
abbots and canons, many tonsured monks.
In God's name they absolved and with the cross
signed all the Frankish dead. Incense and myrrh
they lit, and thoroughly they censed them all.
With every honour then they buried them
and so they left them. What else could they do?     aoi

*The French prepare to return to France:*

### 214

Count Roland's body, Turpin's, Oliver's,
the emperor had carefully prepared.
He watched as each was opened and its heart..
was taken out and wrapped in silk and laid
in a white marble coffer. After that
he had the bodies washed in wine and spice
and then enclosed in deerhide. Next he said
to Theobald, Gebuin, Milo and Otun,
'Put each one in a cart and bring them home.
They spread Galazan silk to cover them.

aoi

*Baligant's vanguard arrives:*

### 215

Just as the king was setting off for France,
the heathen came upon them. Infidels,
the emir's vanguard, filled the way ahead.
Two knights rode out and in the emir's name
challenged great Charles to fight:
                              'Proud emperor,
you cannot leave! The emir Baligant
has come from Araby with all his hosts.
Now we shall see how valorous you are!'

aoi

*The French arm, and array their squadrons:*

### 216

Charles grasped his beard. All his great grief and loss
sprang to his mind, and proudly he surveyed

his fighting men. In a great voice he cried,
loud as he could,

        'My Franks, to arms! to horse!'

aoi

217

At once the emperor armed, donned hauberk, helm,
buckled bright Joyous at his side - a sword
whose light the sun can't dim - and round his neck
hung his Viterban shield. He shook his spear
and mounted noble Tencendur, the horse
he'd won from Malpalin, lord of Narbonne*,
flinging that heathen stone dead from his seat
in battle at the ford below Marsune.
Loosening the reins, he spurred and spurred again,
making the horse bound forward as his men,
a hundred thousand of them, watched their lord.     aoi
On God he called and on the saint of Rome.

218

All across these wide fields the French dismount;
more than a hundred thousand men take arms.
They have swift steeds, good weapons, everything
excellent of its kind. Skilled and alert,
eager to fight, they mount their warhorses.
Bright pennons brush against their shining helms.
Seeing their gallant bearing, Charles called out
to Antelme of Mayence and Jozeran,
count of Provence, and to Duke Naimon,

                         'These
are vassals one can trust! Only a fool,
with troops like these, would worry. Now let's see

whether the Arabs mean to come or not!
If they don't change their minds and beat retreat,
I'll see they pay full price for Roland's death!'
'God grant they come!' Duke Naimon answered him.

aoi

## 219

The emperor called Rabel and Guineman:
'My lords, I order you two to replace
Roland and Oliver. One take the sword
and one the oliphant. Ride out in front;
lead fifteen thousand Franks, the pick of all
our younger men. Then after these will come
as many Franks again, led by Lorain
and my lord Gebuin.' Naimon the duke
and Jozeran array and marshal them.
If they can reach the foe, how they will fight!

aoi

## 220

Franks form these two first squadrons. Next, the third
consists of vassals from Bavaria,
some twenty thousand knights who'll never shirk
the field of battle. There's no race more dear
to Charlemagne, except the Franks themselves,
men who win kingdoms. It's the fighting Dane,
Count Ogier, who must lead such warlike men.

aoi

## 221

Three squadrons has King Charles. Duke Naimon next
arrays the fourth, Germans from Germany,

men of great valour, and, as all agree,
they number twenty thousand. Excellent,
their weapons and their chargers. Fear of death
can never make them quit the battlefield.
These men are led by Herman, duke of Trace,
and he'll die fighting sooner than submit.

aoi


## 222

Duke Naimon and Count Jozeran arrayed
the fifth division. Normans were all these,
and numbered twenty thousand, said the Franks.
Swift are their chargers, excellent their arms.
They'll never ask for mercy! There's no race
in all the world more powerful on the field.
Old Richard is to lead them. Hard he'll strike
in the great battle with his heavy spear.

aoi


## 223

They muster Bretons for the sixth array.
Valiant their thirty thousand warriors ride,
bright spear-hafts painted, banners fluttering.
Oedun, they call their lord. He gave command
to Theobald of Rheims, Count Nevelun
and to the marquis Otun:

     'Lead my men.
The task is yours, I put them in your charge.'

aoi

### 224

Charles has six squadrons ready. Naimon next
arrays the seventh: barons from Poitou
and men of the Auvergne. Well armed and horsed,
these forty thousand knights are placed apart
under a hillside in a valley. Charles
raised his right hand and blessed them. Jozeran
with Godselm will command them on the field.

aoi

### 225

Flemings and Frisians Naimon marshals next;
some forty thousand form the eighth array.
Nothing can make them flinch or leave the field.
'These men will do my service,' said the king.
Rembalt joins Hamon of Galicia
to lead them as knights should against the foe.

### 226

A valiant ninth division now they rank:
Lorrainers and Burgundians, and these
number some fifty thousand. Helmets laced,
bright mailshirts on, they carry heavy spears,
strong and short-hafted. If the Arabs come,
if they dare fight, these men will hit them hard.
Duke Thierry of Argonne commands this troop.

aoi

### 227

The lords of France make up the tenth array,
our finest men, a hundred thousand strong.

Vigorous and well built, their faces fierce,
white hair on head and chin, they wear good mail
of double strength, with swords from France or Spain,
strong shields with many blazons. Now they sit
mounted and eager and they shout, 'Mountjoy!'
With these the emperor rides. The oriflamme
is in the hands of Geoffrey of Anjou.
(This was St Peter's and was called Romaine,
but took its new name from the place, Mount Joy.*)

aoi

### 228

The king dismounted, knelt on the green grass,
turned to the rising sun and urgently
called upon God for help:

'Most holy Lord,
true Image of the Father, now this day
be my defence and shield, as long ago
once you delivered Jonah from the whale
and spared the king of Nineveh and freed
Daniel from torment in the lions' den
and the three children from the blazing fire.
Your love be with me! If it be your will,
God, in your mercy, let me have revenge
for Roland whom the infidels have killed!'

### 229

When he had prayed, the king got to his feet,
marked on his brow the strong and mighty cross
and mounted his swift warhorse. Jozeran
and Naimon held the stirrup. Shield and spear,

heavy and sharp, he took, and sat his horse,
a warrior well made and strongly built,
face bright and joyous, bearing resolute.
Forward he rides, a noble champion.
Before him and behind shrill bugles speak,
louder than all leaps up the oliphant.
The Frenchmen grieve with tears for Roland's death.

*Charlemagne leads his forces towards the enemy:*

### 230

Nobly King Charles rode out. He wore his beard
spread out upon his hauberk; for his sake
the others did the same, and so at once
a hundred thousand Frenchmen could be known.
Tall peaks and towering rocks they passed again,
deep chasms and the dreadful narrow ways,
then left the passes and the wilderness,
and came towards Spain onto the open ground.
Here on a level stretch they took their stand.

*The emir and his men prepare:*

Baligant's messengers return to him;
a Syrian reports:
                                'We've seen the king,
arrogant Charles. Fierce are his men and proud,
they'll never fail their lord. Put on your arms,
battle is imminent.'
                                'Excellent news!'
said Baligant. 'Blow; let my heathen know.'

The heathen drums are sounded, bugles speak,
and all across the host shrill clarions call.
Each man dismounts to arm, and Baligant,
impatient of delay, quickly puts on
his hauberk rich with golden damascene,
fastens his jewelled helmet, hangs his sword
at his left side. This, in his arrogance,
he called by name. He had heard people speak
of Charlemagne's Joyous, so [he said this sword
must be called Precious], and he told his knights
to shout this as a warcry on the field.
His huge broad shield he hangs about his neck;
gold-bossed it is and crystal-rimmed, its strap
made of ring-patterned silk; then grasped his spear,
Maltet, Ill Touch, a weapon whose strong haft
was thicker than a beam, its iron head
a mule-load by itself. Promptly he mounts,
the stirrup held for him by Lord Marcule
who comes from far off lands beyond the sea.
A noble horseman, Baligant! Wide crutch
and narrow flanks he had, deep ribs, huge chest
well formed and shaped, his shoulders broad, his look
fierce and alert. Whiter than may on thorn
in summer time, the heathen's hair curled thick.
His valour's tried and tested many years.
Ah God, how good a knight, if he'd but held
the faith of Christ! He spurred, the bright blood ran;
he set his warhorse bounding, made it leap
over a ditch full fifty feet across.
'This is the man to fight a frontier!'

exclaim the infidels. 'Like it or not,
none of the French can face him and survive.
Charlemagne is mad not to have turned and run.'

### 232

How like a warrior the emir looked!
White was his beard as blossom. In his law
he was most wise and learned; on the field
savage and swift in battle. With him rode
his fine son Malpramis, knightly and brave,
strong, tall and like his forebears.
                                'Sir,' he said,
'I beg you, ride! We shan't set eyes on Charles!'
'Oh yes, we shall,' said the emir. 'Charles is brave.
Many accounts tell of his famous deeds.
But now he's lost Count Roland and he's doomed.
He'll never have the strength to stand our charge.'

### 233

'Fair son,' said Baligant, 'brave Roland's dead.
He was killed yesterday. And Oliver,
valiant and hardy, he was killed as well.
So were the emperor's peers, his cherished twelve.
None of the rest of them is worth a glove.'

### 234

'In actual fact the king is coming back;
my Syrian told me so. With him he brings
ten large divisions. Out before them rides
a very valiant man who blows the horn;

his comrade's bugle rings out in reply.
After them follow fifteen thousand men,
young knights Charles calls his children; after these,
as many more again. These men will fight!'
'Father, give me first blow!' said Malpramis.

aoi

### 235

'Son Malpramis, I grant you all you ask,'
said Baligant. 'You shall attack the Franks
at once. Take Torleu, the king of Persia, take
the Leutiz ruler Dapamort as well.
Halt Charles's arrogance, and you shall have
the whole stretch of my land that lies between
Cheriant and Marquis Valley for your own.'
'My lord, I thank you,' answered Malpramis,
rode forward and received his father's gift.
This was the land King Flurit used to hold.
But afterwards the young man never saw
or took possession of these wide estates.

### 236

Through his great host rode the emir Baligant;
his son rode after him, well made and tall.
Torleu and Dapamort quickly arrayed
thirty divisions, and the least of these
held fifty thousand knights, such wealth of men
the emir could command. The leading ranks
contained the men of Butentrot; next rode
men called Milceni, who all have big heads
and bristles down their backbones just like pigs.

aoi

## 237

Third were the Nubles and the men of Blos;
fourth, Slavs and Bruns; Sorbres and Sors the fifth;
Armenians came sixth along with Moors;
seventh, the men from Jericho; and eighth,
from Nigres; ninth from Gros; lastly and tenth,
the men of strong Balide, and that's a race
who purpose evil always, never good.

aoi

## 238

Emphatically the heathen emir swore
on all Mahomet's powers and on his bones:
'The Frankish king is mad! He's coming on,
he'll have to fight us if he doesn't turn.
He'll never wear his golden crown again!'

## 239

Ten more divisions then they mustered. First
were the hideous Canaanites, who had come
across from the Rout Valley; next the Turks;
third were the Persians; fourth the Petchenegs,
who fight in frenzy; fifth the Soltras came
and the Avar tribe; sixth were the Ormaleus
and Eugiez; seventh were Samuel's men;
the eighth from Bruise, the ninth from Clavers came.
The tenth troop came from desert Occian,
a race who never served Almighty God -
you'll hear of no one wickeder than these.
Their hide is hard as iron, so they need
no helms or hauberks. Violent they are,
bloody and fierce in battle, unafraid.

aoi

The emir ranks ten squadrons: in the first
are giants from Malprose; then next the Huns;
then come Hungarians; the fourth are men
from long Baldise; from Weary Valley, fifth;
the sixth are from Maruse; seventh are Leus
and men from Astrimonie; eighth, Argoilles;
ninth, from Clarbone; the tenth are bearded men
who come from Fronde, a race whom God detests.
The Frankish records list all thirty troops.
Huge are these hosts where countless bugles call!
And now like valiant knights the heathen ride.

aoi

*The emir and his forces ride to battle:*

241

A great and mighty lord is Baligant!
Ahead of him his dragon standard goes;
Mahomet's too and Tervagant's are borne
high in procession. Evil Apollin
is carried there in image. Round them ride
ten Canaanites escorting them, who shout,
'Who wants our gods to heal him, let him pray
and worship them in great humility!'
The heathen bend their heads, bright helmets bow.
'Now you'll all die, you wretches!' cry the French.
'Death and disaster take you! Lord our God,
defend Charlemagne! This fight be in his name!'

aoi

## 242

The emir is a wise and clever man.
He calls his son and the two kings:

                'My lords,
ride out in front, lead all my squadrons. I
shall keep the best three under my command:
Turks, Ormaleus and giants from Malprose...
The men of Occian are to ride with me
and charge Charles and his Franks. If the emperor
encounters me in battle, he will lose
his head clean off his shoulders. That's the best
the Frankish king can hope from me today.'

aoi

## 243

Great are the armies, splendid the arrays.
No hill, no peak or valley lies between,
there is no copse or woodland; none can place
ambush in hiding. Over level ground
the two hosts watch each other.
                'Infidels!'
cried Baligant. 'Now into battle, ride!'
On goes the standard borne by Amborres
from far Aleppo. Loud the heathen yell
their warcry, 'Precious!' and the Frenchmen shout,
'Death and damnation take you!' and 'Mountjoy!'
The emperor's bugles sound, and high above,
louder than all, clear soars the oliphant.
'Charles has a noble host,' the heathen say.
'A long and bloody battle we shall have.'

aoi

Wide is the open plain, spacious the ground.
All over it gold-jewelled helmets gleam,
shields and bright hauberks glitter, spear-points shine,
brave pennons flutter. Shrill the trumpets speak,
high rings the oliphant above them all.
Baligant calls his brother, Canabeus
(who's king of Floredee and holds the land
as far as Severed Valley), pointing out
the emperor's many squadrons:
                                'Look at them!
There go the pride of France. There's Charlemagne -
how gallantly he manages his horse -
there at the rear, leading those bearded men!
Their beards lie on their hauberks, white as snow
that falls on frost. They'll use their swords and spears!
We've a hard fight ahead, a harder one
than any man has witnessed till this day.'
He rode a stone's throw out before his men
and said one word to them:
                                'Heathen, come on!
Follow, I'll show the way!' Grasping his spear,
he brandished it and set the point towards Charles.

                                                        aoi

When Charlemagne saw the emir, and saw too
dragon, ensign and standard borne aloft,
saw all the countless Arab strength spread out
across the whole wide plain, except the place
where his own forces stood - then the king cried:

'My lords of France, you're all fine warriors
and veterans of many a bloody field.
You see those heathen - cowards, criminals!
None of their gods can do them any good.
They're numerous, but what of that, my lords?
The man who doesn't want to ride with me,
let him depart!' Then he spurred Tencendur
so that he sprang four times into the air.
'Ours is a noble king!' exclaimed the Franks.
'Ride, valiant lord, none here will let you down!'

*The great battle begins:*

## 246

Clear was the sky and bright the shining sun,
fair the two armies, vast the great arrays.
The leading squadrons met. Count Guineman
with his companion Rabel slackened rein,
spurred deep and charged full tilt, spears poised to strike.

aoi

## 247

A hardy knight, Count Rabel! Deep he drives
his golden spurs and charges Torleu,
the Persian king. Nor shield nor mail withstand
the powerful blow; into his body runs
the gilded steel and Rabel flings him dead
onto a nearby bush. 'Almighty God
fight for us!' cry the Franks. 'Great Charles is right!
Not one of us must fail our emperor.'

aoi

### 248

Count Guineman attacks the Leutiz king,
shatters the flowery shield, breaks through the mail,
drives the whole pennon's length full into him
and drops him dead, let any laugh or cry.
Seeing this blow, the men of France call out,
'Strike hard, my lords, ride on! King Charles is right,
these heathen wrong! It is Almighty God
who brought us here for justice and for truth!'

aoi

### 249

Malpramis sits a warhorse white as snow
and charges in among the Frankish knights.
Great blows he strikes and tosses slaughtered French
to left and right of him, heaped up in death.
'Listen, my barons!' shouted Baligant.
'I've kept and fed you long. Look at my son
hunting for Charlemagne, how he attacks
one Frank after another! I don't ask
for any better vassal. Infidels!
Ride on, support him! Use your shining spears!"
Now at his word the infidels advance,
hard blows are struck and bloody wounds received.
Bitter the conflict, terrible the strife.
Never before or since has such been seen.

aoi

### 250

Great are the armies, fierce the companies.
All squadrons are engaged. The heathen strike

blows of amazing strength. Ah God above,
how many spearhafts snap and break in two,
what shields are shattered, hauberks ripped apart!
How thickly you'd have seen the ground lie strewn,
the tender grass [all spattered red with blood]!
Again the emir called upon his men:
'My lords, strike at these Christians, strike them down!'
How stubborn was the battle, fierce and hard!
Never has such been fought before or since.
Nothing but death can put a stop to it.

aoi

### 251

Again the emir Baligant cried out:
'Strike them down, heathen, why else did you come?
Noble and lovely wives I'll give you, lands,
honours and fiefs! Strike home!'
                                    'And so we will,
this is our simple duty,' they reply.
Such blows they strike, their heavy spearhafts snap,
more than a hundred thousand swords are drawn.
How close and terrible the conflict now!
Battle indeed he saw, who dared be there.

aoi

### 252

A second time Charlemagne cried to his Franks:
'My valiant lords, you have my love and trust!
How many battles have you fought for me,
how many kingdoms conquered, kings flung down!
I'm well aware I owe you rich reward
in my own person and in lands and wealth.

Take vengeance for your brothers, sons and heirs
whom only yesterday the heathen slew
in Roncevaux! Right's on my side, not theirs,
you know that well!'
                          'That's true, my lord!' they cry.
All twenty thousand Franks who ride with him
as one man promise that no fear of death
nor any pain shall make them fail their lord;
none but will use his lance and drive it home.
Swift they attack again, sharp swords in hand.
Bloody and terrible the battle now.

                                                        aoi

*Death of Malpramis:*

### 253

But through the battleground rode Malpramis,
destroying Frankish knights. Grim was the look
Duke Naimon fixed on him; strongly he charged
and struck the heathen knight. Full through his shield,
through both parts of his hauberk's damascene,
he drove the yellow pennon all its length
into the young man's flesh and flung him dead
down on the ground with seven hundred more.

*Duke Naimon wounded:*

### 254

The emir's brother, King Canabeus,
spurred hard and drew his sword with crystal knob,
brought the sharp steel down high on Naimon's helm
and smashed one side of it, cutting right through
five of the laces; and the hauberk's hood

gave the duke no protection. Through his cap
the steel cut to the flesh, carved off a piece
which fell down to the ground. Naimon was stunned.
Falling he caught, thank God, his horse's neck,
but if the heathen had attacked again,
the great duke would have died. But Charles of France
saw what was happening and came fast to help.

aoi

255

Naimon's in pain and anguish; Canabeus
pressed hard to strike again.
                            'Son of a serf!'
said Charles, 'you'll pay for that!' With all his strength
he struck the heathen, crushed his shining shield
against his heart, drove through throatpiece and throat
and flung him dead; empty his saddle now.

256

Deeply distressed was Charles to see the duke
so badly wounded and his bright blood splash
onto the meadow grass.
                        'Dear lord,' he said,
'good Naimon, ride with me. That wretch is dead,
one spear-thrust and he's gone.'
                            'I'm sure he is,'
said Naimon. 'If I live, you'll see how well
I'll fight for you.' In love and faith they rode
together knee to knee. Beside them fought
some twenty thousand Franks; not one but struck
great blows and fierce against the infidels.

aoi

*French heroes die:*

### 257

Across the battlefield the emir rode
and charged Count Guineman. He smashed his shield
against his heart, pierced chainmail, cut his ribs
free from both flanks so that the count fell dead.
Then he killed Gebuin and then Lorain
and next Old Richard, lord of Normandy.
'Precious is valiant!' cried the infidels.
'Strike, lords, she brings success! Precious will win!'

aoi

*The battle continues; both sides are evenly matched:*

### 258

Ah, could you but have seen the Arab knights
and those from Occian, Argoille and Bascle!
How well they used their spears, how hard they fought!
Nor did the Franks hang back or turn away.
On one side and the other many fell.
The battle raged till evening. Heavy loss
was suffered by the Franks. There will be grief
before the day is ended, fighting done.

aoi

### 259

Bravely and well both Franks and Arabs fight.
Spearhafts and shining spearheads crash and break.
Any who saw those many shattered shields,
who heard steel smash on chainmail, grate on helms,
saw the knights falling, heard the dying men

down on the ground and screaming - such a man
will not forget the agony he saw.
Great strength was needed to endure this fight.
Once more the emir called on Apollin,
on Tervagant, Mahomet -
                              'My great gods;
I have done you good service. Now I'll make
pure golden images for all of you!'                                        aoi
Up rides his aide, Gemalfin, with bad news:
'My lord, the day goes ill. Your son is dead.
Your brother, too, Canabeus is killed.
Two Franks defeated them, and one of those
I'm sure was Charles the emperor, tall, well made,
beard white as April blossom.' Baligant
bowed down his helmet, hid his face; such grief
he thought would kill him instantly. He called
his vassal Jangleu of Outremer.

*Baligant knows he cannot win:*

### 260

'Jangleu, come here,' he said. 'You've courage, sense,
and long experience. I've always known
I could trust your advice. Arabs and Franks,
how do you see the battle, shall we win?'
'You're a dead man,' said Jangleu. 'Your gods
can't give you any help. King Charles is proud
and his knights valorous. I've never seen
such fighting men as his. But call once more
upon the lords of Occian, on the Turks,
the Arabs, Enfruns, and the race of giants.
As for what comes of it, why, let it come!'

*Baligant leads a heroic charge:*

### 261

On his broad chest the emir spread his beard,
white as the hawthorn blossom. Come what may,
he does not mean to hide. Then loud and shrill
he set a bugle to his lips and blew
a clear high note that all his heathen heard.
His squadrons rally all across the field:
the men of Occian whinny and bray,
the Argoilles give tongue like hounds. Careless of harm,
into the thickest of the Franks they charged
and broke their ranks. Full seven thousand men
they struck and killed in that assault alone.

*Duke Ogier rallies the French:*

### 262

No trace of cowardice Duke Ogier knew,
no better fighter ever put on steel.
He saw the Frenchmen break, and called at once
to Geoffrey of Anjou and Jozeran,
to Thierry of Argonne, and angrily
shouted to Charles:
                        'Look how the infidels
are cutting down your men! See how they die!
Please God you never wear your crown again
if you don't charge at once, wipe out your shame!'
None of them spoke a word; they spurred, slacked rein;
where they could find the heathen, there they struck.

Hard blows and fierce Charles gave; Duke Naimon too,
Count Geoffrey, standard-bearer, and the Dane,                    aoi
fighting Duke Ogier. What a knight he was!
He spurred and raced full tilt to strike the man
who bore the dragon-standard. Down they went,
Amborres and the dragon, down as well
went the emir's royal standard in the dust.
Baligant saw them go, Mahomet's sign
and his own standard too. Now first he thought
he could be in the wrong and Charlemagne right.
The Arabs faltered and slackened their attack.
King Charles called on his kinsmen once again:
'Barons, in God's name, will you help me now?'
'No need to ask us that!' exclaimed the Franks.
'Be damned to any coward who hangs back !'

                                                                 aoi


*Charlemagne and Baligant meet:*

### 264

Day passed and evening fell. Heathen and Franks
still struck, still fought and struggled. Valiant men,
the leaders of these hosts! Neither forgot
to shout his battle cry: 'Precious!' cried one,
'Mountjoy! Mountjoy!' the other, famous cry!
Each knew the other by his loud clear voice.
There in the middle of the field they met
and mighty blows emir and king exchanged.
Spears pierced ring-patterned shields, drove through
                                                    chainmail,
but neither man was wounded. Saddle-girths

parted and saddles slipped and both kings fell.
Swiftly they rose, drew swords, fiercely attacked.
Nothing but death can part these combatants.

aoi


### 265

A very valiant fighter, Charles of France,
nor does the emir fear him or hang back.
They draw their naked swords, exchange great blows
each on the other's shield. Leather and wood
they hack to pieces, wooden lining too,
so that the studs fall out and bosses break;
on unprotected mail they place their blows
and from the shining helmets strike out sparks.
This cannot end till one admits he's wrong.

aoi

*Baligant calls on Charles to surrender; Charles asks Baligant to accept
the Christian faith; both refuse:*

### 266

'Charles,' said the emir, 'think! Now be advised,
deal with me differently. You've killed my son;
against all right you're trying to take my land.
Become my man, do homage, you shall have
the whole of it in fief. Come and serve me
from this land to the east!'

                              'A foul disgrace!'
said Charles. 'I may not love or live in peace
with infidels. Do you accept God's law,
the faith in Christ he gave us, then indeed
I'll be your friend at once. Then serve and trust
God, the almighty king!'

'Poor preaching, that!'
said Baligant. They took their swords again.

aoi


*Charlemagne is wounded; Gabriel intervenes:*

### 267

Enormous strength has the emir Baligant.
He strikes Charles on his helm of shining steel,
cracks it apart and, where the hair is short,
slices a piece of flesh from off his skull,
a handsbreadth wide or more, so that the bone
shows through, naked and bare. Under this blow
the emperor staggered and he almost fell.
But God wants Charles alive, victorious,
not dead and beaten; up came Gabriel
and said to him:
                   'What are you doing, Charles?'

*Death of Baligant:*

### 268

Charles heard the angel's voice, lost every fear,
regained his strength; alert and vigorous,
he struck the emir with the sword of France
high on his helmet where bright jewels blazed.
Down through his head he cut and spilled his brains,
down through his face to where the white beard grew,
and flung the emir stone dead to the ground.
'Mountjoy!' he shouted, summoning his men.
Duke Naimon heard, caught hold of Tencendur,
remounted Charles. The heathen turned and fled,

as God above intended them to do.
And now the Franks have won their heart's desire.

*The French pursue and slaughter the fleeing enemy:*

### 269

The heathen flee, as God Almighty wills.
Hard on their heels, emperor and Franks pursue.
'My lords,' said Charlemagne, 'avenge your grief!
Relieve your hearts and minds. Early today
I saw the tears you shed.'

                                   'My lord,' they said,
'this we must do!' Each man hard as he could
struck mighty blows and cut the heathen down.
Only a very few of them escaped.

*Death of King Marsile:*

### 270

The heat was great and dust rose up in clouds.
The heathen fled, the Frenchmen harried them;
right to the city walls they ran them down.
Up her tall tower Queen Bramimonde had climbed,
taking her clerks and canons, men who served
that false unholy law God cannot love,
who wear no tonsures and are not ordained.
When the queen saw the Arabs overthrown,
she cried aloud,

                        'Mahomet be our help!
Ah, noble king, our forces are destroyed!
Disgrace and sorrow, Baligant is dead!'
Marsile heard this, turned to the wall and wept,

covered his face and of pure grief he died.
Disaster triumphed and he gave his soul
into the hands of devils come from hell.

aoi

*The French hold Saragossa:*

### 271

The infidels are killed, a few have fled,
and Charles has won his battle. He commands
that Saragossa's gates should be destroyed:
no one will hold the place against him now,
he's sure of that. He takes the citadel,
his forces enter in and that night lie
as conquerors there in triumph. Proud indeed
is the old king, white-headed, white of beard!
The queen surrendered to him all the towers,
ten great and fifty smaller ones. Success
comes to the man whom God himself befriends.

*The townspeople are christened or killed:*

### 272

Day passed and dark night fell. The moon shone clear.
Over the conquered town the burning stars
flamed in the heavens. By their light, the king
ordered a thousand Franks to search the town,
ransack the mosques and all the synagogues.
Axes they used and sledgehammers and smashed
all images and idols, broke them up.
No sorcery or falsehood must endure.
The king trusts God and wants to do his will:
his bishops bless the waters; into them

they lead the infidels to be baptised.
If anyone opposed the king's command,
he had him hanged or burned or put to death.
More than a hundred thousand infidels
by baptism became true Christian souls -
all but the queen, for Bramimonde must go,
so the king wished, a captive to sweet France
and there through love she should convert to Christ.

*Charlemagne leads his army home, taking his prisoner Queen
Bramimonde with him:*

### 273

Night passed and daylight dawned. Charles garrisoned
the towers of Saragossa, placing there
a thousand warlike knights, men who would hold
and keep the city for the emperor's use.
Then the king mounted, as did all his men.
So did his prisoner, Bramimonde the queen.
Charles means no harm to her, nothing but good.
Joyous and jubilant they set off home,
forced their way past Nerbone* and reached Bordeaux.
Here on the altar of that valiant man,
St Severin, Charles put the oliphant,
but first he filled it full of gold *manguns*.
Pilgrims who visit there can look at it*.
On the great ships that lie in the Gironde
he crossed the river, brought his sister's son
ashore at last at Blaye; brought Oliver,
his noble comrade, brought the archbishop too,
Turpin, the brave and wise. He had these lords
placed in white tombs and there at St Romain

the three companions lie. To God above
and to his Names the Franks commended them.

*Reaching Aix, Charlemagne summons his judges for the trial of
Ganelon:*

By hill and vale rode Charles; he would not stop
until he came to Aix, but still rode on
till he dismounted at his palace steps.
There from his lofty hall he sent out men
to call his judges: Saxons, Frisians,
men from Bavaria and from Lorraine
as well as Germans and Burgundians,
Poitevins, Normans, Bretons and the best
and wisest of the men of France herself.
And now began the trial of Ganelon.

*Death of Alda:*

274

King Charles is back from Spain, he reaches Aix,
the noblest seat in France, and climbs the steps
up to his palace. There inside the hall
coming to meet him was the noble girl
Alda the beautiful. She asked the king:
'Where is your captain, Roland, my betrothed?'
In grief the emperor wept and plucked his beard.
'Sister, dear child, the man you want is dead.
Instead I'll do my very best for you:
you shall have Louis, what more can I say?
He's my own son and he'll hold all my lands.'
'I cannot grasp your meaning,' Alda said.
'God and his angels and his saints forbid

that I should be alive if Roland's dead.'
She lost all colour, fell at Charles's feet
and died there where she lay. God rest her soul!
The Frankish barons mourned and wept for her.

### 275

Alda the fair is dead, her life is done.
The king thought she had fainted. With deep grief,
weeping, he bent to pick her up, but then
her head rolled loose, and clearly she was dead.
He sent at once to fetch four countesses
and had her corpse borne to a nunnery,
where it was watched all night till daylight dawned.
Close by an altar there they buried her
with every honour. Reverence and respect
the emperor paid to Alda's funeral rites.

aoi

*The trial of Ganelon:*

### 276

Charlemagne the emperor has come home to Aix.
Before his palace in the citadel
in heavy irons stands vile Ganelon.
Serfs lashed him to a stake and bound his hands
with deerhide thongs, and then they thrashed him hard
with clubs and cudgels, as he well deserved.
There in great pain he waited for his trial.

### 277

It's written in the ancient history
that the emperor summoned men from many lands

to gather at his chapel there at Aix.
A high and holy day it was, the feast
of valiant St Sylvester, so they say.
Here now begins the hearing and the plea
of Ganelon, he who betrayed the Franks.
Charles has the traitor dragged into his court.

aoi

*The charge against Ganelon: his defence:*

278

'My barons,' said Charlemagne, 'now do me right
against this Ganelon! One of my host,
he came to Spain with me and robbed me there
of twenty thousand of my Franks. Through him
I lost my nephew, whom you'll never see
live on this earth again, lost Oliver,
the brave and courteous knight, lost the Twelve Peers.
All these he sold for gain.'
                                    'Let me not hide,'
said Ganelon, 'the facts! This is the truth:
that Roland injured me, both over gold
and other property; I sought his death.
The charge of treason, though, that I reject.'
'We will consider this,' replied the Franks.

279

There stood Count Ganelon before the king,
handsome and tall, bright colour in his face,
in all apppearance a most noble knight,
if he had but been true. He looked around,
looked at the Franks, the judges and his kin,

thirty of whom had come to stand by him;
then loud and high he shouted,

'In God's name,
barons, let me be heard! Listen, my lords -
in love and faith I served in the emperor's host.
Count Roland hated me, sent me to die
a painful death as envoy to Marsile.
I used my wits and lived! And I defied
Roland the warrior, and Oliver
and all their comrades too. Charles himself heard,
so did his noble lords. Vengeance I took,
I did indeed, but treason I deny.'
'We will withdraw,' the Franks said, 'and confer.'

*Pinabel, Ganelon's kinsman and champion:*

### 280

Ganelon, watching his great trial begin,
had thirty kinsmen with him. One of these
was Pinabel, to whom the rest deferred,
lord of strong Castle Sorence. He was skilled
in speech and word play, and in arms as well.

aoi

### 281

'You are [my only hope],' said Ganelon.
'Deliver me from death and from this charge!'
'You'll be released at once,' said Pinabel.
'No Frenchman here will sentence you to hang,
or else the king will set us face to face
and with my sword I'll prove the man a liar.'
Count Ganelon fell at his kinsman's feet.

*Charlemagne's men are reluctant to face Pinabel:*

## 282

The Saxons, the Bavarians and Franks
withdrew for consultation. With them went
Normans and Poitevins and many knights
from Germany; Teutons were there as well;
polished and courteous, the Auvergnats.
The thought of Pinabel subdued them all.
'Better to let it go,' each said to each.
'Call off the trial, and then we'll ask the king
to drop the charge against Count Ganelon
as at this time. In future let him serve
Charlemagne in love and faith. Roland is dead.
None of us here will see him any more.
No gold or other wealth will bring him back.
Only a fool would challenge Pinabel.'
Not a man there dissented, but for one:
Lord Geoffrey's brother, Thierry of Anjou.

aoi

## 283

His barons now returned to Charles and said,
'My lord, we ask you to acquit the count,
in faithful love to serve you from now on.
Give him his life, for he's most nobly born.
Death can't bring Roland back, and there's no fine,
no payment that will give him back to us.'
'You have betrayed me, all of you!' said Charles.

aoi

*Thierry of Anjou challenges Pinabel:*

### 284

All the king's men had failed him. Seeing this,
Charles sank his head into his hands and raged,
exclaiming at his grief. Out stepped a knight,
Thierry, Duke Geoffrey's brother, from Anjou.
Thin, slight and sparely made, not tall
although not overshort, he had black hair
and a dark face. Now courteously he said,
'My lord, fair king, do not distress yourself.
You know I've served you long. My ancestors
give me the right to champion such a plea.
Whatever wrong Roland did Ganelon,
yet he was in your service and this fact
should have protected him. In selling him
Ganelon broke his word and oath to you;
he is forsworn and guilty. He should hang,
his corpse be used like that of any man
committing such a crime. If he has kin
who challenge this my judgment, here's my sword,
and readily I will uphold my words.'
'Well said, well spoken!' said the Frankish knights.

### 285

Out before Charles came Pinabel, a knight
strong, tall and valorous, fast on his feet.
None takes a blow direct from him and lives.
'My lord,' he said to Charles, 'this court is yours.
Tell them to make less noise! And Thierry's here,
his judgment given - I tell him it is false!

I'll fight with him to prove it.' Then he gave
his righthand deerskin glove to the emperor.
'I want good sureties,' said Charlemagne.
The thirty loyal kinsmen pledged their faith.
'I,' said the king, 'will be his pledge to you.'
He has them guarded till the law's fulfilled.

aoi

### 286

When Thierry saw that he must fight at once,
he gave his right glove to the emperor
and Charles by hostage offered guarantee.
He had four benches brought into the square,
and there the combatants now took their seats.
The challenges were all correctly made;
the observers all agreed. Ogier the Dane
made the arrangements for the battle. Next
the two require their horses and their arms.

*The two champions prepare:*

### 287

Now that it is decided they shall fight,          aoi
both make confession, are absolved and blessed,
hear mass, receive communion and make
rich offerings in the churches where they pray.
Then they appeared before the emperor,
spurs on their heels, their strong light hauberks on,
bright helmets closed and golden-hilted swords
hung at their sides. About their necks were slung
their quartered shields, and each in his right hand
grasped his sharp shining spear. They mount swift steeds.

For Roland's sake a hundred thousand knights,
weeping, shed tears for Thierry of Anjou.
Almighty God knows what the end will be!

*1e combat begins:*

### 288

Below the town of Aix broad meadows lie.
Here the two men encounter. Both are strong,
valiant, experienced, their horses swift,
active and agile. Deep they spur, slack rein
and then with great force strike. Shields fly apart,
bright hauberks gape, girths snap and saddles slip
and fall onto the ground. The watching knights,
a hundred thousand men, see this and weep.

### 289

Both champions are down. Swiftly they rise.                aoi
Strong Pinabel is light and very fast.
The two confront each other now on foot
and with their golden-hilted swords they cut
and rain down blows each on the other's helm.
So hard they strike they cut the metal through.
How the French knights lament, how they exclaim!
'Ah God,' says Charlemagne, 'make clear the right!'

*bel offers generous terms if Thierry will yield:*

### 290

Pinabel spoke: 'Thierry, admit defeat!
I'll do you homage; all I have is yours.
Take what you like, but reconcile the king
and Ganelon!'

'I cannot think of it,'
Thierry replied. 'May I be held accursed
if I agree to that! Let God decide,
let him make clear which of us two is right.'

aoi

*Thierry calls on Pinabel to surrender:*

### 291

And Thierry spoke:
                    'Come, Pinabel, you're brave,
strong, tall, well made, and all your comrades know
how valorous you are. Give up this fight!
I'll make your peace with Charles. On Ganelon
such justice shall be done, no day will pass
when it's not talked about.'
                              'May God forbid!'
Pinabel answered. 'I'll support my kin,
all of them, always. There's no man alive
can make me fail in that. I'd rather die
than suffer such disgrace.' Again their swords
hammer on jewelled helms and sparks fly up
and blaze into the sky. Nothing but death
can end this battle, separate these two.

aoi

*Thierry is wounded:*

### 292

A mighty man of war was Pinabel.
On Thierry's helmet from Provence he struck;
fire flashed from it and set the grass alight.
Setting his swordpoint full on Thierry's brow,

he drew it downwards through his face and cheek -
his right cheek was all bloody - and cut down
right through his mailshirt over the abdomen.
God intervened and would not let him die.

aoi

*Death of Pinabel:*

### 293

Thierry could feel the wound there in his face,
saw his bright blood splash on the meadow grass;
on Pinabel's shining steel helm he struck
and split it to the nosepiece. Out he spilled
the brains inside his head, thrust to one side,
flung his opponent dead onto the ground.
This blow had won his fight. The Franks cried out,
'This is the work of God! Clearly it's right
for Ganelon to hang. His kinsmen too,
who came to stand beside him in his trial.'

aoi

### 294

The moment Thierry's victory was won
the emperor ran to him, as Naimon did,
with Geoffrey of Anjou, Ogier the Dane
and William lord of Blaye. Charles took the knight
into his arms and wiped his wounded face
with his great marten furs; then put these off
and let his men put others on him. Next
with tender care they helped Thierry unarm
and put him up onto an Arab mule.
Nobly escorted, joyful he came home.

They came to Aix, dismounted in the square.
The killing of the others now began.

*Execution of Ganelon's sureties:*

## 295

Charles called his counts and dukes and said to them:
'These men I'm holding, what do you advise?
It was to stand by Ganelon they came,
they're pledged as sureties for Pinabel.'
'Not one of them shall live,' they answered. Charles
gave orders to his officer, Basbrun:
'Go hang them all on the accursed tree.
By this white beard, if one of them escapes,
you shall be hanged yourself.'
                              'And so I should!'
replied Basbrun, and with a hundred men
he dragged the thirty off and had them hanged.
He who betrays kills more men than himself.

aoi

*Execution of Ganelon:*

## 296

Germans, Bavarians, men from Poitou,
the Bretons and the Normans now returned.
Much more than all the rest, the Franks insist
that Ganelon must die a dreadful death.
Four chargers were led out, the traitor's hands
and feet made fast to them. Strong beasts they were,
swift, spirited. Four servants held their heads.
Close by a piece of water in a field
this man was sent to hell. His sinews stretched

and lengthened, all his limbs tore from his trunk;
on the green meadow grass his bright blood ran.
Count Ganelon has died a felon's death.
No one must sell his friends and boast of it.

*Conversion and baptism of Queen Bramimonde:*

### 297

His vengeance done, Charles called his bishops in,
German and French and from Bavaria:
'A noble lady captive in my house
has had enough instruction and now wants
to trust in God and be a Christian.
Baptise her, so that God may have her soul.'
'She must have godmothers,' the bishops said,
'[honoured and noble women].' This was done.
Great was the company that gathered there
around the baths at Aix, where they baptised
the queen of Spain and called her Julian*.
True understanding gave her Christian faith.

*Gabriel summons Charlemagne to a new task:*

### 298

King Charles had done his justice, had assuaged
his mighty anger and had seen the faith
of Christ set firm in Bramimonde the queen.
Day passed and dark night fell. Charles lay in bed
in his high vaulted chamber. Gabriel
came to him now from God and ordered:
                              'Charles,
summon your empire's forces, fight your way

into the land of Bire and go to Imphe,
relieve King Vivien from the heathens' siege.
The Christians there cry out to you for help.'
Charles had no wish to go there, none at all.
'Ah God,' he cried, 'a weary life I lead!'
He wept for grief and plucked at his white beard.

Here ends the story told by Turoldus.

# NOTES

Laisse 3
'At Michaelmas' represents *a la grant feste seint Michel del peril*. The description of Mont-S-Michel on the Normandy coast as being *in periculo maris*, 'within the danger of the sea', became attached to the saint's name regardless of geography.

Laisse 28
St Peter's Pence was a tax paid from England to Rome, first recorded under Cnut and revived in 1076 by William I.

Laisse 48
A mangun was a gold coin worth two bezants.

Laisse 68
*Note 1.* In this poem only the infidels have drums. Terror had been struck into Christian hearts by 'the new secret weapon, the terrifying roll of their drums' used in southern Spain in 1086 and 1090 by Berber warriors from Morocco
(Trend, *Language and History* p.67).

*Note 2. La tere certeine e les vals e les munz. Certeine* is here taken to mean 'level', but it may be a place name, Cerdagne. However, the high Pyrenean area of this name lies too far east for the heathen barons to have ridden through it on their way from Saragossa to Roncevaux.

Laisse 92
'Mountjoy', the French warcry, may have derived from the name of the *mons gaudii*, the hill of joy, from which pilgrims had their first sight of Jerusalem. See also laisses 183 and 227.

## Laisse 94

'The land from Balbiun to Atliun' in the ms reads *la tere datliun e balbiun*. Editors have emended this phrase to produce a reading referring to two Old Testament characters who deservedly 'went down alive to Sheol' (Numbers XVI). However Boissonnade makes a good case for trusting the ms reading and interpreting these as the names of places in Syria, not of persons (*Du nouveau* p.224).

## Laisse 111

*Seint Michel del Peril* may refer to Mont-S-Michel on the Normandy coast or possibly to a village near Roncevaux. Saintes stands on the Charente about 70 km SE of La Rochelle. Besançon, capital of the Franche-Comté, at this period was part of the Empire. Wissant is a Channel port between Calais and Boulogne.

## Laisse 112

'Exploits of the Franks' translates *la geste francor*, ie the *Gesta francorum*, Deeds of the Franks. We do not know whether this refers to an actual work or not.

## Laisse 121

In medieval times there was a town called Africa on the coast of Tunisia, destroyed by the Spaniards in 1541; or the reference may be to Roman Africa, now Libya.

## Laisse 155

No one survived the battle; St Giles must have been present in spirit.

## Laisse 172

'His private property' freely translates *que il teneit sa cambre*. See Whitehead p.135 where he explains that the word 'chamber', normally referring to the part of a castle kept for the lord's private use, can also refer to land which paid its revenues direct to him for his personal expenditure.

## Laisse 183
This refers to the famous Holy Lance discovered in Antioch in 1098 at a time when the crusaders were in great need of reassurance.
For 'Mountjoy', see laisses 92 and 227 and notes.

## Laisse 189
'Babylon' in medieval usage meant the town we call Cairo. This emir came from Egypt. He represents, as the references to antiquity, Homer and Virgil make clear, all the power of the unsaved, unchristian past rising up to challenge Charles after he has defeated the contemporary threat offered by Islam. As we shall see, the emir is a noble figure and displays to the full the pagan virtue of fortitude.

## Laisse 190
Jewels were believed to possess magical powers. A carbuncle was a 'little coal', a red ruby-like stone which was thought to give light of itself.

## Laisse 192
'And from the starboard side stepped into Spain' is a new rendering of this vexed line. It and the one before it read:

*Li amiralz est issut del calan*
*espaneliz fors le vait adestrant.*

Most commentators take *espaneliz* to be a person's name and have thus invented 'a Saracen baron' in attendance at the emir's right hand. This seems unlikely, because in every other instance in the text when a new character is introduced, a brief identification is given - eg 'an infidel called Climorin', 'a king called Corsalis,' 'the heathen Esturgant' and so on. Nor does this supposed Saracen baron ever appear in the story again. While struggling with this line I also happened to be reading William Golding's *Rites of Passage* and came to the burial at sea where the body 'was placed with its feet towards the starboard, or honourable side, by which admirals and bodies and suchlike rarities make their exits'. This surely does help. Sir William was kind enough to explain to me that the starboard or steer-board side of the ship was the honourable one because that was where the master stood to steer his vessel. Cargo, less honourable, went ashore from the other, the larboard side. The emir, *li amiralz*, would certainly have disembarked from the honourable side, but I confess that I do not see how to reconstruct the line in order to wring this meaning out of it.

### Laisse 206

A Pyrenean plant around which such a legend may have grown up is the De Candolle orpin (*mucizonia sedoides*), a red-leaved stonecrop, patches of which can look like pools of blood.

### Laisse 208

*Cum en espaigne venis mal seignur.* Bédier supplies *a* before *seignur*, and interprets the phrase to mean: 'With what an evil lord you came to Spain!', ie that Charles is reproaching himself for Roland's death.

### Laisse 217

Narbonne, in the text *Nerbone*. Boissonnade thinks that neither this *Nerbone* nor that of laisse 273 can be identified with Narbonne, but with some unidentified Saracen stronghold, possibly Arbona (*Du nouveau* p.126).

### Laisse 227

The oriflamme was the banner of the kings of France and kept at the abbey of St Denis outside Paris. It is here confused with a different banner, that of the city of Rome. See laisses 92 and 183 and notes.

Laisse 273

*Note 1:* The French are travelling from Saragossa to Bordeaux, so that this *Nerbone* is certainly not the Narbonne on the Mediterranean coast. See note to laisse 217 above.

*Note 2:* 'Pilgrims who visit there ...' This reminds us of the importance of the pilgrim routes, the competition between different monastic houses for pilgrim trade and the part played by such houses in the creation of the chansons de geste. It may not be over-imaginative to link this line with the episode in laisse 170 when Roland uses the oliphant to kill an infidel, and then remarks that he has cracked it across the bell and broken off all the gold and crystal. Perhaps the oliphant on display on St Severin's altar in Bordeaux did not quite measure up to pilgrims' expectations.

Laisse 297

Many explanations are put forward for the choice of the name Julian or Juliana for the Spanish queen. The likeliest is still that of Bédier: that she is named for a fourth century saint whose relics were believed to lie in the monastery of Santa Juliana in northern Spain. This grew into a village, now Santillana del Mar, and is one of the stopping places on the pilgrims' way to Santiago de Compostela.

Also published by Llanerch:

Anglo-Saxon Verse Runes
Louis Rodrigues

Beowulf
John Porter

Taliesin Poems
Meirion Pennar

Maid Marian
Thomas Love Peacock

Faereyinga Saga
F. York Powell

Studies in Early
Celtic Nature Poetry
Kenneth Jackson

Names from the Dawn
of British Legend:
Taliesin, Merlin, Aneirin, Arthur
Toby Griffen

For a complete list of c.200 titles, small-press
editions and facsimile reprints, write to Llanerch
Publishers, Felinfach, Lampeter, Dyfed, SA48 8PJ.